Bath Bramble

Dawn Aldridge Poore

D1560166

ZEBRA BOOKS
KENSINGTON PUBLISHING CORP.

Chapter One

The Honorable James Williford, recent heir to the distinguished title of Viscount Atwater, sat rather carefully behind the massive walnut desk piled with bits of paper and several rather large envelopes that bore tradesmen's names. He ignored the papers and concentrated on slowly closing his eyes without groaning. He was not successful. He moaned and held his head as the knocker banged out front, the sound reverberating from one side of his head to the other. His condition was not assisted by the jaunty entrance of his best friend, the Honorable Percy Golightly. To compound James's misery, Percy was whistling merrily.

"For God's sake, will you stop that infernal racket?" the Viscount whispered hoarsely, putting his hands over first his eyes, then his ears.

Percy brought up a very fine quizzing glass and peered at his friend. "What's this? Not all the thing today, are you, Jamie? Thought you might have downed a few too many last night."

Since this reproach failed to elicit anything more than a deep groan from the Viscount, Percy tried another tack. "Are we still on to go to Tattersall's today? I've been counting on it."

"*Uuuhhhh.*" It was a moan from the Viscount. "Good Lord, Percy, I can't move, much less go to Tattersall's." He put his head down carefully on the desk, pillowing it on some especially large, thick envelopes.

"But you promised." The tone was accusing. "And we're to meet Beckley to inspect that chestnut of his I'm thinking of buying. I've already made the arrangements." Percy stared at his friend without a trace of compassion. "We're supposed to leave right after you have your appointment with old Pettigrew."

"Pettigrew!" James gasped as he jerked his head up, then stopped in agony and put his hands against his temples. "Oooohh," he moaned. "Lord, Percy, I had forgotten all about old Pettigrew. I can't do it—I can't talk to the chap. I don't care how important it is. Confound it, Percy, I'm a sick man."

"Well, I know just the cure," Percy answered, putting aside his tan doeskin gloves and his ebony cane. "Got to get you in shape. I intend to make it to Tattersall's this afternoon." He left the library, calling out instructions for the butler and banging the door behind him. The only response was another low moan of pain from the Viscount.

A half hour before it was time for Mr. Oswald Pettigrew, solicitor, to arrive, the impossible had been accomplished—the Viscount was more or less coherent, albeit somewhat pale. He was also full of strong, bitter coffee and a particularly vile concoction Percy had mixed from his own recipe. "Cure you right away," Percy had said, as James had choked and tried to spit it out. Whatever it was, it had been completely terrible to taste, but it worked. As soon as he was able to speak again, James informed Percy that he had only managed to exchange a headache for a stomachache.

After Percy's ministrations, James had managed to make it upstairs where his valet, Packard, had dressed him and made sure his cravat was tied just right. His dark brown hair had been carefully arranged in a windswept, and even his eyes had, through the magic of some vile green drops produced by Packard, changed from bloodshot to their usual warm brown. All in all, by the time the solicitor arrived, the Viscount had managed to change into the very picture of a sedate young gentleman of the *ton*.

James sat down again at the walnut desk. "I feel like the devil," he said to Percy, who was whistling again.

Percy peered at him through his quizzing glass. "No matter," he said. "As far as Pettigrew's concerned, you look every inch the prosperous Viscount. Cut this visit short if you can, and we'll get on to Tattersall's. Beckley won't wait long for us."

"Stay in here if you want," James said. "I've no secrets from you." He scattered the papers on the desk.

Percy shook his head. "Old Pettigrew won't say a word until I leave, and you know it. The soul of discretion, he is, and as stiff and formal as they come. I'll wait in the yellow parlor." He gave James a wave and disappeared through the door, nodding a cheerful good morning to Pettigrew as they passed.

Mr. Pettigrew walked in slowly and looked around with distaste. His gaze lingered on the large stack of envelopes that had been shoved to the back of the desk. He was carrying another batch of them under his arm.

"Good morning, milord," Pettigrew said stiffly, sitting

down and giving the Viscount a rather derogatory look.

"Morning, Pettigrew," James said, noticing the solicitor's gaze on the envelopes on the desk. He tried unsuccessfully to stuff them into a drawer. "To what do I owe the pleasure, Pettigrew? I was going to arrange a meeting with you soon, so your note requesting a visit was quite convenient."

Pettigrew made no attempt to erase the frown from his face as he removed one envelope from the stack he carried and placed the remainder on the desk. "This has brought me here, milord," he said. "You seem to have quite exceeded your allowance, and I am being besieged by tradesmen who know I manage your affairs."

"I knew I was a little under the hatches," James remarked, shuffling the stack, "but not by much, all things considered." He stopped and grimaced. "Confound it, Pettigrew, can't you do anything to get me out of this legal mess?" The lawyer managed a disapproving sound as James rushed on. "That was what I wanted to talk to you about, anyway," the Viscount said, waving a hand vaguely toward the bills. "Can't you break my father's will or something? It's ridiculous for me to be Viscount Atwater and still be on an allowance like a schoolboy." He paused. "There are some things I need to do."

"Your father wished his will written that way, and I merely wrote it to his specifications," Pettigrew said. "It cannot be broken."

"I'm of age," James said stubbornly. "Good Lord, I'm *past* being of age — I turned five-and-twenty this year. I should be allowed to make full use of my inheritance. This 'quarterly allowance' business is embarrassing. Everyone in London knows you have me by the purse strings." James stood and began pacing the floor. "Can't we say that poor Papa was temporarily out of his mind?"

Pettigrew gave him a chilly look. "Do you really want it bandied around the *ton* that your father was ready for bedlam? Besides, if I were asked, I would have to say that the late Viscount was quite sane and capable of managing his affairs."

"No — you're correct," James said with a sigh, "I wouldn't want everyone thinking he wasn't quite right in the head — although, mind you, I don't think he *was* where this will is concerned." He continued to pace and then hit the side of the desk with his fist, wincing at the noise. "What I *do* object to, Pettigrew, is my father trying to run my life from the grave." He paused and made a face. "And he's doing a very good job of it, too."

"Milord," Pettigrew said, "I don't think your father was trying to run your life. . . ."

"Oh, yes he was. And he did. From the time I was in leading strings to the time I was shipped back home from Oxford, he was constantly after me." He glared at the solicitor. "I can't tell you the number of times he called me irresponsible. Me, of all people!" He paused and looked out the window. "Nothing I ever did was quite good enough."

Pettigrew shifted uncomfortably. "I'm sure, milord, that your father merely had your best interests at heart. The conditions of the will are but temporary, if you recall."

"Oh, I recall well enough," James said bitterly, sitting down in the large chair behind the desk. "I'm to be Viscount Atwater and to inherit everything, but it isn't going to do me any good until I'm thirty because you control all the funds." He glared at Pettigrew. "Do you realize how difficult it is to be pressed constantly for

money? There are things I'd like to do, things that —"
He broke off and said no more.

"According to the terms of the will, there *is* a solution,"
Pettigrew said, ignoring James's last remark. "Your father felt that what he termed your 'irresponsibility' could
be cured. If you recall, he was a great believer in the
steadying influence of marriage; so once you marry, you
will be able to do as you wish with your fortune."

"Dash it all, Pettigrew, I don't happen to be irresponsible." His mouth set in an angry line as he shook his
head. "Besides, I don't want to get leg-shackled!" There
was an uncomfortable moment of silence, then James
continued, "Anyway, all the girls I meet here in London
are looking either for a fortune or for some dandy to
squire them around." He paused a moment. "Or else
they're completely Friday-faced," he added with a shud-
der.

"Uuummm." Pettigrew stared at him from under
bushy brows. "If you don't marry," he said in a ponder-
ous, final tone, "then you will be on an allowance until
you're thirty. The terms are very plain." He cleared his
throat and changed the subject. "Milord, there is the
matter of your bills. . . ."

James looked down at the pile before him and the par-
tially open drawer stuffed full. "A gentleman must have
a few necessities, Pettigrew," he said. "Surely you realize
that."

"A half-dozen pairs of brown gloves, as well as a half-
dozen pairs of black ones? Two pairs of black hessians just
this quarter? The cravats? And the expense of the horses
and the equipage — a new carriage *and* a new curricle?"
Pettigrew picked up another bill as though it burned his
fingers. "*And* silver-studded harness?"

"Everything seemed to fall apart at once; besides, my father wouldn't have wanted me to go about looking shabby," James said, his jaw set. "And I'm not going to do it, Pettigrew. A gentleman has to have some standards."

"Just so," Pettigrew answered, "and your father provided what he thought to be an ample allowance."

James fixed him with a stare. "I have other expenses which are nobody's business but my own."

"Quite so, milord," Pettigrew said hastily, realizing he was close to overstepping his bounds, "and I believe arrangements might be made on most of the items, except perhaps the curricle, but there is the small matter of these other debts." Pettigrew paused. "I'm speaking of your vowels at the clubs, milord."

"Oh, good God, I had forgot that," James said. "I went on something of a binge that whole month, but I haven't even been to the clubs since . . ." He paused.

"Since last week," Pettigrew reminded him, pulling out a dated slip. "At White's, I believe."

James made a face. "I might have been there, but I wasn't gambling—at least, not very deep. As for last month, I did lose quite a bit. I can't even remember the amount."

"A very large amount, milord," Pettigrew said, his bushy gray eyebrows drawing together. "I regret to tell you that I have been forced to discuss this matter with the other trustees of the will, and we have concluded that strict measures must be instituted. We are unable to draw more than the will allows to cover your debts, so you're going to have to pay these amounts out of your allowance." He paused at James's angry expression. "Milord, there *is* no other course. The trustees have no

11

choice — we must insist that you put yourself on a strict budget. We have drawn up a list of what expenses we believe essential." He handed James what looked to be a very short list.

James glanced over the few items and paled. "This is ridiculous, Pettigrew. I can't live and keep my household on this. Besides, I told you that I have other private expenses."

"I'm sorry, but you must limit yourself to this amount," Pettigrew answered, ignoring his expression. "As to the payment of your debts, I suggest that you cancel some of your trips to Scotland, and I'm sure you'll also be able to raise some cash by selling a few of the things you've purchased recently. I suggest you try to sell the carriage and the curricle, as well as the horses you bought last month. Actually, I have already investigated this avenue, and I'm pleased to tell you that Lord Westeley, one of the other trustees, has graciously offered to take the horses off your hands."

"Graciously!" sputtered James. "Graciously, you say! Pettigrew, I'm telling you that those are prime pieces of horseflesh. Westeley hasn't been able to get his hands on anything like that in years." He jumped up from the chair and glared at Pettigrew. "I won't have it, Pettigrew! I tell you I won't! I refuse to sell everything I've purchased and retire like a common pauper. Furthermore, Westeley won't touch my horses! There's got to be some way around the conditions of that blasted will!"

"There aren't," Pettigrew said shortly, and, it seemed to James, with enjoyment. "The only way you'll control your inheritance is to marry or reach thirty, whichever comes first."

"Then, by God, I'll get married!" James paced the floor in agitation.

Pettigrew wasn't perturbed. "That is entirely up to you, milord." He waited until James stopped pacing and had collapsed back into the desk chair. "There is one other small matter, milord."

James grimaced. "What now, Pettigrew? Who else needs a pound of my flesh?"

"Hardly that." Pettigrew tried unsuccessfully to hide a smile. "This concerns your wards."

"My wards?" James looked blank, then remembered. "Oh, you mean that confounded Callie Stone and her brat of a brother. Lord, what now? I thought I specifically asked that you send them money regularly. They should be well fixed."

"That has been done," Pettigrew said, displaying an envelope for James to see. "However, Miss Stone has written a very agitated letter to you. She seems to feel that your presence is required as someone needs to take what she terms 'a firm hand' with her brother." Pettigrew's expression left no doubt that James's hand would not be firm enough.

"A firm hand? Lord, why doesn't she just birch the lad? As I recall, he was just a little stripling anyway."

"Mr. DeQuincey Stone is now twenty and is currently rusticating at home after having been sent down from school," Pettigrew said dryly. "I believe it would prove quite difficult for Miss Stone to birch him."

"Twenty!" James looked at Pettigrew in surprise. "Are you sure? I thought he was ten or so, but then I haven't seen Dee since his father died." He paused and reflected. "I suppose he is that old," he said in surprise. "I saw Callie for a few minutes at Papa's funeral last year, and I

13

hardly knew her. Lord, she must be, let's see, three-and-twenty now." He looked at Pettigrew in amazement. "Good Gad, Pettigrew, she ain't even been presented or anything. Do you mean that poor girl's on the shelf and you haven't done anything about it? She should have been out years ago!"

"I discussed this matter with you, milord, when your father died. If you recall, you told me not to bother you as you had other pressing concerns, but that I should do whatever Miss Stone wanted."

"I did?"

"You did," Pettigrew said firmly. "I told you at the time that both your father and I had done everything we could to have Miss Stone come to London for a season, but she refused. She has some idea that she is, ah . . ." There was a significant pause. "She wishes to be a *painter.*" Pettigrew said the word with distaste.

"A *what?*" James said. "A painter? So Callie's dabbling in paints? What's wrong with that, Pettigrew? Most of the girls I know dabble in watercolors and such."

Pettigrew shook his head. "Miss Stone wishes to be an *artiste.* She refuses to come to London, refuses to meet any eligible young men, refuses to engage in any social activities whatsoever except for those that concern her brother or her family."

James made a face. "Sounds as if Callie needs taking in hand more than her brother does. Callie always was headstrong, if I remember correctly. As for Dee, he's probably just a high-spirited schoolboy annoying Callie as usual."

"She does not specify the problem, milord, so it may be more than that." Pettigrew handed him the letter. "However, my involvement is merely as a messenger —

Miss Stone advises me that she has written you twice and received no reply, so she asked me to pass this along to you personally."

"Twice? I haven't read the mail since I got back from Scotland." James shuffled through the envelopes on his desk. "I thought I saw a familiar name on one of these. No matter, I'll read it later." He took the envelope from Pettigrew. "Lord knows how I'll fob Callie off on this one. I can't exactly take charge of a boy only five years younger than I am." He tossed down the envelope without opening it. "I'll think of something, I suppose."

"If you wish to view the situation for yourself, Miss Stone and her brother are in Bath."

Jamie raised an eyebrow. "Been there for a while, haven't they? Didn't they move there after their father died? As I recall, their mother had relatives there. I haven't seen Callie since, except for that moment at the funeral." His face wore a pensive look. "We had some high old times when we were children, you know. Callie followed me around like a puppy, and we were in one scrape after another, right up until the time her father died. It's a shame I haven't seen her since."

Pettigrew did not answer, and James quickly came back to reality. "I'll try to get down there — if I can afford it," he added with a tight smile. "Right now I seem to be a little dipped."

To James's satisfaction, Pettigrew's face reddened. "I believe the trustees would agree to paying for your trip to Bath, since it concerns your wards."

James stifled a smile and forced himself to adopt a flippant tone. "Famous, Pettigrew, but will I have to starve once I get there? I'll need to keep my curricle for the trip — with the horseflesh, of course — and the carriage for the luggage, and I'll need rooms for myself and my man, as well as expenses. Bath can be damnably dear."

"Avoid running up any excess expenses and I see no problem," Pettigrew said bluntly, refusing to be baited. "I'll advance you what the trustees consider enough. Let me know when you plan to leave." With that he stood. "May I call on you again soon to discuss what the trustees have budgeted? That will give you time to go over the list and amounts. Perhaps by then you'll know when you'll be leaving for Bath."

A few seconds after the door closed behind Pettigrew, Percy knocked and entered. "That front room's devilishly warm." He stretched and yawned. "I almost went to sleep waiting for you to finish up with old Pettigrew. How did it go?" He took one look at the expression on James's face and poured him a rather large brandy. "Bad news?" he asked as he cleared a small space on the top of the desk and placed the snifter in front of his friend.

"There's no way to break the terms of the will," James said, absently stirring the brandy with his finger.

"Are you sure?"

James nodded. "Pettigrew is the soul of integrity. If he says there's no way, then there's no way." He picked up the snifter and drained the brandy. "I'm to be put on a budget."

"I don't believe it."

"It's true. Pettigrew wants to come back soon so I can agree to the sums. Look at this list." He shoved the list toward Percy, knocking a letter off as he did so.

Percy picked up the letter and glanced at the frank. "Miss Callista Stone. Where have I heard that name?"

"My ward," Jamie said briefly. "Callie Stone."

16

Percy frowned. "I should know her, and I remember the name, but I can't place the face. Has she come out recently, or is she a small child?"

Jamie laughed aloud. "You'd remember her if you'd seen her. Tall, slender, reddish hair, dark blue eyes. Her father was Matthew Stone, the man in partnership with my father on the woolen mills. When old Matthew died, my father became guardian to Callie and her brother, DeQuincey."

"Wait a minute — I believe I've met Miss Stone. Quite attractive, as I recall."

"Callie?" James looked incredulous. "An all right girl, but I don't think I'd call her attractive. More of a termagant, I'd say.

"I must have the wrong person in mind, then." Percy shrugged. "Did you say her brother was named DeQuincey? Named after your father?"

"Yes." With a wave of his hand, James dismissed the subject. "What am I going to do about this money business, Percy? I wish you had to endure this mess — why did your grandmother have to leave you enough for you to have whatever you want?" He sighed. "Lord, all you have to do is snap your fingers and you have funds, while I . . . it don't even bear thinking on, Percy."

Percy grinned at his friend. "Hardly that, but as to the money, Grandmother knew what a trustworthy soul I would become."

"*You? Trustworthy?*" James snorted audibly, then sighed. "Percy, what am I going to do about this? Pettigrew says the only way I can come into my inheritance is to turn thirty or to marry, whichever comes first."

"If you hadn't spent all that money last quarter . . ."

Jamie shook his head. "I had to do it, Percy. The tenant houses were falling apart at the country estate."

"And I suppose it was necessary to spend a small fortune upgrading the houses for all those Scotsmen who work at the mill?" Percy chuckled.

"Certainly it was! How can people work if they don't have a decent place to stay? I put MacKenzie in charge and told him to spend whatever was necessary." James sighed. "I just didn't realize that so much would be necessary. I spent my entire year's allowance on that, so I've had to run on tick for everything else. I even had to borrow money to pay the household wages." He paused and ran his fingers through his hair. "Damn!"

"Why don't you tell Pettigrew? Tenant houses are a legitimate expense for the estate. Besides, you really don't spend as much as I do on personal items. I'm certain Pettigrew would approve of you spending money on the estates."

James made a face. "I know he would, but I won't give Pettigrew or the other trustees the satisfaction thinking Papa's will was reforming me. They'd feel too virtuous."

"So now you can feel poor and virtuous." Percy grinned at him.

"Touché." James smiled back. "Now, since you read that so well, tell me how to solve my problems now without appearing responsible."

"It would seem to me that you have only one choice, Jamie my friend, but I don't believe you care to get leg-shackled."

James looked glum. "It's come down to that, Percy. I don't have any other choice. It seems that the only thing I'm to be able to choose is the lady. For my money, there ain't a good one in all of London."

There was a grim silence in the library. Finally Percy

spoke. "There's always the eldest of the North sisters, what's her name?"

"Oh, Lord, you don't mean Prudence?"

"That's the one. She'd be perfect. If you have to marry someone, you should get a meek, biddable girl, one who would retire to the country and leave you alone. You'd need only see her occasionally during the season and on holidays."

"All right, that's the kind of girl I need, but please, Percy, not Prudence. She's so meek I'd never know she was around. Besides, she squints."

"You can't have everything," Percy observed. There was another silence. "What about Magdalen Pierce? Her mother's a dragon, but she's biddable enough."

"I can't stand her mother," James said glumly, "and the poor girl looks remarkably like a horse I once had."

The silence lengthened, punctuated by James's sighs. "There's absolutely no one who ain't already been spoken for, Percy. It's hopeless."

"True. We might as well go on to Tattersall's."

James glared at him. "How can you think of Tattersall's at a time like this?"

"Easily. I promised Beckley that . . ." Percy stopped and snapped his fingers. "I know — Venetia Bramley!"

"Venetia Bramley?" James made a face. "Lord, Percy, she's a spoiled brat, even though she *is* a beauty." He reflected a moment. "That might not be too bad, though. I hear she needs to marry a fortune." He thought some more and then shrugged his shoulders. "No, Percy, it wouldn't work — not at all. I need what money I can scrape up for myself instead of marrying some chit and having to pay off all her debts." He looked sorrowful. "She is a beauty, though." There was another pause. "I wonder how much her father's debts total. If it wasn't too much . . ."

"Her mother's a dragon, too," Percy said, interrupting. "But as to your question—I don't think her father owes too much—it's just that he doesn't have a feather to fly with. You might be able to do it, Jamie."

"It's a thought." James leaned his chin on his fist, "I wouldn't hurt to make inquiries, would it? I'd go see her right away, but I think she's out of town. I wonder if she's going to be gone for a while."

Percy made a face. "Think about this one seriously, Jamie. Venetia Bramley may look good on your arm, but she'll be expensive. One of the reasons her father's under the hatches is because he's indulged her every whim."

James waved him aside. "Lord, Percy, I'm just going to make few discreet inquiries, and perhaps pay a call or two on Miss Bramley." He looked smug. "Once I discover where she is," he added.

"I happen to know where she is," Percy said somewhat reluctantly. "It seems that she and her mother have gone to Bath to take the waters. The mother has an ailment of some sort . . . bad temper, probably."

James disregarded everything except the important part. "Bath?" he asked quickly. "Did I hear you say Miss Bramley was at Bath?"

Percy nodded. "Down there for the next month, so I hear." He gave James a startled look. "Surely you ain't planning on traveling to Bath to court the lady? Jamie, listen to what I told you—the reason her father's under the hatches is because Miss Bramley spends like there's no tomorrow. I'm sorry I mentioned her name. I don't know what I was thinking. Let me give it some more thought — there's plenty of fish in the sea."

"Too late now," James said with a chuckle. "I think you might have hit on the perfect solution. Miss Bramley would be more than presentable, and perhaps she wouldn't bother me too much. And besides, I need a wife, any wife, and I need one as soon as possible. I'd planned to go to Scotland to meet with MacKenzie to talk about reworking the mills and getting some new machinery. That'll be costly."

"I'm telling you, if you're thinking of marriage, Venetia Bramley ain't the one for you. You'd spend all your time taking care of her every whim, besides spending a small fortune on whatever took her fancy. Not only that, you'll never get Venetia to the country unless somebody's having a house party." He frowned at his friend. "No, take my word for it, you'd do better with someone else."

James shook his head. "Right now, it looks as if Miss Bramley will be the one to entangle my heart."

"Bosh. It's the challenge of the thing. The only thing entangling your heart is your purse strings. I'm telling you, Jamie . . ."

James stood and waved aside his objections. "I'm going to Bath to see Miss Bramley, Percy. My mind is quite made up." He smiled sunnily at his friend. "Besides, if Miss Bramley don't work out, I'm sure Bath will be full of eligible ladies. You can already count me a married man — and, considering my inheritance, a rather wealthy one at that."

"Well, you ain't wealthy now, not by a long shot, so just how do you plan to go? You just told me that you hadn't a feather to fly with and were on a budget. A place in Bath don't come cheap."

"Taken care of," James said gleefully. "And I can kill two birds with one stone. Good heavens, Percy, a pun!"

Percy stood and looked doubtfully at him. "A pun? James, was that brandy too much for you?"

"No, really, a pun. Stone—my ward. Callie Stone wanted me to go Bath to talk to her brother, and old Pettigrew agreed for the trustees to finance the trip." He walked around the desk, humming. "Things are looking up, Percy, I can feel it in my bones. A coincidence like this doesn't just happen—it's fate . . . the hand of Providence smiling on me." He grinned at Percy. "You *are* going with me, aren't you?"

"I don't think the hand of Providence ever smiled before. Are you *sure* this is the right thing to do?"

"Of course it is—I'm telling you, it's fate."

Percy looked resigned. "I don't have anything else to do, and I suppose I should. Maybe I can save you from making a complete cake of yourself."

"Nonsense." James laughed. "I tell you, Percy, this was meant to be. I'll go see Pettigrew tomorrow, get enough funds to see us two or three weeks, and then we're off to Bath!"

Chapter Two

Miss Callie Stone walked rapidly across the room and jerked the drapes back from the tall windows. "Still raining," she said dully, watching the rain fall in heavy sheets and sluice across the paving stones in front of the Pulteney Street residence. "It's rained in Bath every day this week." She turned back to the small fire, warming her hands. "I'm glad you came by, because I'm at wit's end. I'm ready to give up on Atwater," she said to her companion. "I wrote twice and didn't hear from him, so I wrote Papa's solicitor, Pettigrew, to see if he could do anything." She sat down and rang for tea. "I don't know if that will do any good or not."

"Callie." The word was a strangled sob.

Callie looked quickly from the fireplace to her friend. She got up and sat down beside her. "Oh, Venetia," she said, putting her arms around her, "I'm such a goose. Here I am spending all my time worrying about Dee, while you're having such problems. I'm *so* sorry."

"Callie," wailed Miss Venetia Bramley. "It's so awful!" With that, she broke into a fresh spasm of tears, not dainty little tears, but big, gulping sobs that shook her all over. "Oh, Callie!" she wailed again. The maid brought in the tea tray, and Callie nodded to her to put it on the table. Meg scowled briefly as Miss Bramley moaned again, put the tray down with a thud, and left. Callie waited until the door was safely shut.

"Venetia, please," she said, soothingly. "Here." She handed Miss Bramley a cup of strong tea, heavily sugared. "This will make you feel better." She watched as Miss Bramley sipped at it. "Drink it all," she insisted. "How can you tell me what's wrong if you're crying so hard? There, that's better."

Miss Bramley mopped at her eyes with a tiny lace handkerchief. "What would I do without you, Callie?" she said with a wavering smile. "Since that first day at school when you took up for me, I've depended on you."

Callie smiled at her. "That's what you should do, Venetia," she said, pouring each of them another cup of tea. "Am I to take it that there's another problem with the dashing Captain Sinclair?"

Venetia's face crumpled and she started to cry again. "Stop that now, Venetia," Callie said sternly. "Just tell me what's wrong. Last week, if I recall, he had spoken longer than was necessary with a Miss Mincell, but I thought that contretemps had been nicely resolved. Only yesterday, you told me that Captain Sinclair had declared his love for you right in the middle of George Street. I believe you said that your life was now complete."

"Oh, he does love me," Venetia said in a trembling voice, "and, Callie, I love him so much. But it's Papa."

"Oh." Callie had wondered how Venetia's family

would regard Venetia's infatuation with Captain Andrew Sinclair, currently of the Scots Guards. He was a handsome, fine-talking gentleman, who had some expectations, but right now, he was poor as the proverbial churchmouse. "And did the captain speak to your father?" she asked.

Venetia nodded. "That's the problem. It was terrible, Callie. . . . he came this morning and there was a horrible scene with Papa. Papa . . ." she paused and gulped. "Papa all but chased him out of the house!" This last ended on a wail. "Whatever will I do?"

Callie bit her full lower lip. "There's nothing to be done right now. You and Captain Sinclair will have to accept your father's verdict until the captain's prospects improve. Didn't you tell me he was due to inherit from an uncle?"

"Yes, but that don't signify at all! He won't inherit until forever!" It was another wail. "Callie, you've never been in love! I can't *live* without Andrew!" Venetia indulged in another bout of tears that took Callie several minutes to stop.

"Exactly what *did* your father tell Captain Sinclair?" Callie asked when Venetia was finally quiet. "Did the captain ask permission to visit you?"

"He offered marriage," Venetia said between hiccups. "And we're going to get married, Callie, I swear it. I love him." She rubbed at her eyes with her handkerchief.

"And what did you father say to him, exactly?" Callie asked quickly, hoping to forestall more tears.

"Papa lied," Venetia said baldly. "He told Andrew that I was already betrothed to another — a gentleman of title' was the way Papa put it." Venetia gave her a guilty glance. "I didn't get to hear any more because Mama came by and chased me away from the keyhole." She paused. "I saw Andrew leaving, and I could see that he was very angry. I know he thinks I lied to him about not being attached to anyone except him." There was another silence. "I sent Dulcie to him with a message that I would meet him this afternoon."

"You didn't!" Callie could only stare.

Venetia lifted her chin defiantly. "Yes, I did. Callie, I love Andrew and I'll never love anyone else. I intend to marry him."

"Venetia, please consider what you're doing. If you meet Captain Sinclair without your father's permission, your reputation will be forever compromised."

Venetia tossed her head, her blonde curls falling down around her face and framing it. "I don't care." Her face crumpled again "Oh, Callie, whatever will I do?" she wailed.

Callie patted her shoulder ineffectually. She glanced up as her Aunt Mary looked into the room and gave a questioning look. Callie nodded yes as her aunt pointed upstairs, then turned her attention back to her sobbing friend. "Venetia, please don't cry. We'll think of something, I promise."

Venetia lifted her ravaged face. "Do you really think so?"

"Yes," Callie said, though she knew there was no solution at hand. "Why don't you go upstairs and wash your face? I'll have Meg bring you some cool water and cucumber slices for your eyes. You'll feel better."

Venetia stopped crying and touched her swollen eyelids. "You're right — I must look a fright." She got up and started out of the room as Callie rang for Meg.

At the door she turned and tried a wavering smile. "Whatever would I do without you, Callie?"

Callie watched Venetia follow Meg out of the room. "The poor widgeon," she said to herself with a sigh.

A few minutes later, Callie heard the knocker clang. She waited for either John or Meg to answer it, but in a minute or so it clanged again, even more insistently, and she could hear the faint sound of someone speaking loudly outside. The tone of the voice was not happy. Callie belatedly remembered Meg was upstairs attending to Venetia, and John had been sent on one of Aunt Mary's numerous errands. She straightened her hair and mopped at the wet spot left by Venetia's tears, then went to the door herself. She opened the door just as the knocker was being lifted again, and a dripping, sopping body fell in on her.

"Whatever . . . ?" she muttered, shoving the very wet gentleman away. He appeared to be someone she had never seen before. "You must have the wrong address," she said frigidly as she gave him another shove out the door and shut it soundly in his face.

The knocker clanged again, this time accompanied by a shout. "Callie, drat it, let me in!"

In amazement, Callie opened the door and regarded the half-drowned gentleman facing her. Carefully she took him in, from the tips of his muddy hessians to the top of his head, now covered with dripping brown curls that were plastered to his forehead. Her blue eyes widened in surprise as she recognized him. "Jamie!" she shrieked, "Jamie, you've come at last!" She threw her arms around is neck, squishing his cravat audibly. "Mr. Pettigrew wrote that you probably wouldn't be here, but I *knew* you couldn't let me down. I just *knew* you'd come! I told Aunt Mary that you wouldn't let us down." She paused for breath and then let go, looking down at the wet front of her gown.

"I'm drenched," he offered as an unnecessary explanation.

"I'm not one to say I told you so, but I said you should have ridden in the carriage with me," Percy said, "though nothing would do except for you to make an entrance into town in that curricle."

"Do you always have to be so damned *right?*" James asked, gritting his teeth. "How did I know it was going to flood the entire countryside?"

"Well, there were clouds, and those thunderheads . . ."

Callie had vivid memories of Jamie's short temper, so she hastily interrupted Percy. "You got my letter about Dee and you've come to help . . . how very splendid of you, Jamie."

James stood dripping and uncomfortable, guilt written plainly on his face. "Dash it all, Callie, you should have known I'd be right here as soon as I knew you needed me. I couldn't let you down." He gave Percy a glare as Percy coughed discreetly. "I had planned to get here much sooner, of course, but, um, there was something of an emergency that took a great deal of my time." He put his hands on Callie's shoulders and stood in front of her so she couldn't see Percy's amused expression, but then he held her at arm's length as his own expression changed to one of complete amazement. "My lord, Callie, you've changed!" He stood back a little and took his turn looking at her intently from the top of her curly auburn hair to the tips of her yellow kidskin slippers, clearly amazed at how she had changed into a very fine woman indeed. "I don't believe I would have recognized you," he said slowly. "Callie, you . . . Callie, I . ." He stopped, still gazing at her, and let his words trail off.

"You haven't seen me in a while," Callie said, with a dimpled smile that lit up her dark blue eyes. "A rather long while."

A guilty flush suffused the Viscount's face as he finally forced himself to stare instead at the carvings on the door. "Well, dash it all, Callie, I've been busy."

She laughed. "I know what your 'busy' entails, Jamie. I'm sure there've been shooting parties and," she paused, "whatever."

He looked offended. "Actually, I've been involved with the estates and the tenants, and," he grinned engagingly at her, "whatever." He stopped, caught his breath, and sneezed. "Callie, I'm drenched and about to freeze to death. Are you going to make me stand out in the street forever? If I don't get warm and dry, I'm going to come down with the grippe."

Callie stood in the doorway, arms akimbo. "I want to know something first, Jamie—did you come to Bath to talk to my brother? I do hope you did." There was a stubborn set to her generous mouth. "I wrote to Mr. Pettigrew that Dee needed you. You *must* take him in hand."

"Yes, yes, yes!" Jamie shouted. "I'll talk to the lad. I'll do whatever you want." He sneezed again and raindrops flew. "Just let me in out of this infernal downpour. I'm not going to do either you or Dee any good if I die from a chill."

Callie moved aside and then shut the door behind the men. "Did you get this wet just coming here from your rooms?" she asked, watching the water drip from James's clothes and puddle on the floor. "I didn't realize it was raining *that* hard."

"Rooms," Percy said with disgust. "Tell her about the rooms, James."

"I'll work it out, Percy," James answered with exasperation. "I always do." He forced a cheerful expression and then turned to her with a smile. "Callie, I know it's been a while since I've seen you, and you know I'm not really one to impose on hospitality, but . . ." He stopped, searching for the right phrase.

"Yes?" Callie prompted. There was a long silence.

"We need a place to change clothes, and it's either here or James's Aunt Cavendish's house, and I vetoed that," Percy said, resignation tinging his voice as he mopped ineffectually at his waistcoat. "The agent won't be able to get us rooms until next week. We're going to have to find somewhere to stay until then."

James turned to Percy, drops of water flying. "Dash it all, Percy, I said I'd take care of it. We *did* rush right down here, and I'm sure the agent's letter must have crossed us on the way."

Percy rolled his eyes upward and Callie, seeing Jamie's temper seething, interrupted. "Do you want to change here? We've plenty of space and you're perfectly welcome to use a room upstairs."

Jamie sighed and clasped her hand. "I knew you wouldn't mind, Callie. I told Percy so." He gave Percy a look of smug satisfaction which his friend ignored. "My man's outside in the carriage with my clothes. I'll call him." He started for the door, slipped in a puddle of water, and slid back toward the stairs, grabbing frantically at the railing to keep from falling. He finally managed to come to a stop, the top of his body draped over the banister.

"My goodness, is that you, Viscount Atwater?" Venetia asked, tripping down the stairs. She paused on the step above James's dangling head and looked down at him. "I hardly recognized you!"

James pulled himself up and stood at the bottom of the steps, still dripping gently. "Miss Bramley," he said in a choked voice, tossing the end of his cravat across his shoulder, splashing Callie generously. "I'm delighted to see you."

"And I you," Venetia answered, smiling at him. Her face showed no trace of her tears. "Are you visiting Bath, milord? Have you come to take the waters? I hope you're not ill."

"Ill?" James collected himself and searched for his reasons to be in Bath. "My ward. Uh, yes, I've come to Bath to see about my ward. He's, um, somewhat ill, I believe."

Miss Bramley frowned slightly and looked at Callie. "You didn't tell me that Dee was ill, Callie."

James looked from one to the other, aghast. "You two have made each other's acquaintance?" he asked faintly.

Callie laughed. "Why else would Venetia be here? I've caught you, Jamie. Dee's only illness is his ill temper." She turned and rang for Meg. "Why don't you summon your man and get out of those clothes? You truly *will* be ill if you don't. As for your friend . . ." She paused.

Percy finally broke the silence. "Percy Golightly," he

said, introducing himself. "Sometimes James ain't too big on the social amenities," he added with a grin.

"How could you say such a thing, Percy?" James demanded. "You told me you remembered Callie, so I thought the two of you had been introduced. I *knew* you had met Miss Bramley. Besides," he added, "I was right in the way of making introductions."

Percy's answer was halted when a short, plump woman entered, pausing to look at them all. "Good heavens," she said, "whatever has happened here?" She stared at the puddles on the floor.

"Aunt Mary," Callie said, "do you remember Viscount Atwater?"

"Yes, and I believe I've heard you mention his name lately," Aunt Mary said, her glance taking in all of James's shortcomings.

James glanced at Callie with an impish grin. "I'm sure it wasn't in a complimentary way."

Callie gave him an insulted glare. "I would never be uncomplimentary." She paused. "Well, perhaps a little." She grinned back at James and turned to her aunt. "Jamie's come to Bath to see about Dee. He — Jamie, that is — got caught in the rain and doesn't have a place to stay."

"Well, as part of the family, of course you'll stay here. We have more room than we need." Aunt Mary's tone brooked no opposition.

"As much as I appreciate your offer, Percy and I couldn't possibly impose on you that much, Mrs. Uh . . . uh . . ." To his complete horror, James couldn't remember her name.

"Elliott," murmured Callie under her breath.

"Mrs. Elliott," he said with relief. "That is, I certainly would never infringe on the family connection. I wanted only a place to change into dry clothes. Percy and I plan to take rooms at the White Lion until next week, when our lodgings will be ready."

"Nonsense," said Aunt Mary briskly. "You would neither be imposing or infringing. I *insist* on your staying here with us. Callie needs the company, and Dee will be glad to have someone close to his own age around." She rang again for Meg and headed for the back of the house, calling for the servants. "Have your man take your things upstairs—Meg will show you where," she said over her shoulder as she walked away.

"I can't . . ." James began, but Callie interrupted him.

"You might as well give up. When Aunt Mary makes up her mind, your only option is to do as she says. There's no refusing her."

James glanced at Miss Bramley, a look which Callie intercepted. "Venetia is visiting me just for the afternoon," she explained. "We're very close friends. She's staying with her family in Gay Street."

"Really?" Percy gave James a significant glance, which James ignored.

"I'm delighted to hear that." He gave Venetia a brief smile, then turned his full attention back to Callie. "Your aunt may be right, Callie," he said, looking at her from top to toe again. Staying here may be the best thing after all." With a smug and satisfied smile, he went to the door and signaled Packard to bring in their trunks.

Upstairs, the servant unpacked and had James into dry clothes in a very short while. James was whistling merrily and putting the finishing touch—one rather

33

plain fob—to his ensemble when Percy came in. "You were right, Percy. Coming to Bath was an inspiration." He gave himself a satisfied nod in the mirror.

"Yes," Percy agreed. "Not many people would welcome us so."

"I know." He whistled softly through his teeth. "Percy, did you see the way she smiled at me?"

Percy nodded. "Very friendly."

"I tell you, I had no idea this was going to happen. I was completely unprepared."

Percy looked perplexed. "You didn't know what was going to happen? Staying here? She seemed as much a dragon as your Aunt Cavendish, I thought. I realize Mrs. Elliott has a nice smile and was very friendly, but . . ."

James interrupted him. "Whatever are you talking about? I was speaking of love." He sighed. "Did you see how she looked at me? Could this be love, Percy? As I recall, you've been in love a thousand times."

"Take my word for it, James—you're not in love. I'm an expert in these things."

James laughed and glanced in the mirror again with a satisfied smile. "I own that you are, Percy, but I'd have to admit that I've never looked at a woman before and heard wedding bells."

"You're probably catching a cold in your ears from being out in all this rain. I've had a ringing in my ears from that myself. You can rule out wedding bells."

"All right, for the time being, although if I hear them again, I'll have to think about some things seriously."

"Two people have to hear wedding bells for it to mean something," Percy observed, "and I didn't hear any."

"You don't count," James said flippantly. "Besides, I'm telling you, I've seen that look before—I think she's interested."

"Oh." Percy paused. "In what?"

"In me, you booby. I'd be willing to lay odds that I'll be an engaged man inside a week. For certain in two."

"Fifty pounds says you won't."

James looked wounded. "I can't believe you said that. You saw how she looked at me. I can't miss."

"I think perhaps she was simply amazed at your appearance," Percy said. "It ain't often you see a drowned man walking around."

James looked sadly at the pile of sodden clothing Packard had put aside to clean. "My second best waistcoat, too." He shook his head and grinned at Percy. "If I had that effect on her when I was a sartorial mess, just think what I'll do to her now."

They started down the stairs together. Percy stopped stock still in the middle of a step. "Love?" He laughed and looked at James. "You, in *love?* I'd like to see the reaction at the clubs if they heard that one. Wedding bells!" He laughed again.

"Ssshh." James looked around hastily and flushed a bright pink. "I might as well announce something in the *Chronicle* as confide in you, Percy. Watch your tongue."

Percy raised an eyebrow. "Love? Not you. Besides, there's no such thing. You've told *me* that every time *I've* been in love."

The Viscount sighed. "I knew you'd make me eat

35

my words."

Percy chuckled. "And to think I'm in for fifty pounds. I'll tell you what, James, much as I hate to kiss fifty pounds good-bye, I'll help you all I can."

James looked horrified. "Thank you, but no, Percy. I know what disastrous results your help can lead to. Remember the time you tried to help me in Paris?"

"You mean the milkmaid who . . . ?"

"Ssshh." James glanced down at the door where voices could be heard. "I'll do my own courting, if you please." He listened as he heard Callie and Venetia laugh, and a small smile lit his face. "Let's go down and get reacquainted, shall we?"

As they reached the bottom of the steps, Callie and Venetia came out of the small drawing room. Venetia had on her cloak. "Ah, Jamie, an improvement, I must say," Callie said, looking at him. "You weren't at your best playing the part of a water spaniel."

"Unfair, Callie," Venetia answered as she fastened her cloak and tied her bonnet ribbons. "Viscount Atwater is always a handsome gentleman."

"Are you leaving, Miss Bramley?" Percy asked. "I had hoped you might stay a while." He gave James a knowing glance which James ignored.

Venetia smiled prettily at the two of them. "I must go, but I wanted to extend an invitation to you to visit us at your convenience. Callie and I spend a great deal of time together, and your company would be most welcome." With that, she turned to bid Callie good-bye and left.

"I do believe you're right," Percy murmured to James as they went into the drawing room. "She does seem interested."

They waited in the small room until Callie returned from seeing Venetia out. The small fire in the parlour dispelled the gloom and damp chill, making the room altogether inviting and cozy. James collapsed into a chair in front of the embers, negligently crossing his legs. "That heat feels fine on a cold, damp day," he said as Callie gave him a cup of tea, then handed one to Percy.

"I'll just wait outside," Percy said.

Callie smiled at him. "I'm hardly going to confide state secrets to Jamie. Please stay."

"Besides," James said with a laugh, "what I know Percy knows and vice versa." He sipped appreciatively. "This is wonderful." He stretched and smiled at her. "Callie, you can stop worrying now. Exactly what is the problem that's been bothering you?"

"I'm worried about Dee," she said without preamble. "Aunt Mary and Venetia both tell me that I'm all in alt over nothing, but Dee's all I have left except for Aunt Mary and some assorted cousins."

James sipped at his tea. "People usually get too worried over children's pranks and moods."

"Children?" Callie stared at him. "Good heavens, Jamie, Dee's hardly a child."

James frowned. "Now that you mention it, Pettigrew told me Dee was, let's see, twenty now." He looked up in amazement. "I can't believe that—it seems like only yesterday he was following you and me around. He was barely out of leading strings."

"I'm three-and-twenty myself, Jamie," Callie noted, "but at twenty Dee thinks he's grown, and he isn't at all. I suppose I've spoiled him because . . ." She stopped and began again. "At any rate, he won't listen to me any longer. Since he was sent down from school . . ." She paused and put down her tea.

"Pettigrew mentioned that in passing, too, and I found it hard to believe as well. I hadn't realized he was old enough to be away at school. What did he do?"

Callie caught her lower lip between her teeth and fought down a blush. "I'm not really sure, but from what I can piece together, it seems to have involved a dancing bear and an innkeeper's daughter. I don't know in which order."

"That's all right," James said hastily. "I'll find out from Dee. It was probably just a young man's scrape. Most of us have had them at onetime or another."

Callie nodded. "I could understand that, but there's more. Jamie, if Dee goes, I don't know what I'll do. Papa wanted him to run the woolen mills, but Dee wants to go away and leave them."

"Go? Where to?"

"That's the whole problem," she wailed. "He's got his mind set on emigrating to America. He read a book by Dr. Franklin, and now Dee has quite made up his mind to go to Philadelphia and explore the frontier or some such." Her expression was anguished.

James paid close attention to his teacup while he tried not to grin. "I'll talk to Dee," he said with a straight face. "I'm sure I'll be able to change his mind."

"I hope so." Callie looked sharply at him. "You think I'm being silly, don't you? Jamie, you don't realize what this means to me. If Dee goes to America, I'll be all alone. Papa's dreams will have been dashed, and Mr. MacKenzie will die from apoplexy."

"MacKenzie? Do you mean Angus MacKenzie?"

James laughed aloud. "Callie, I've met dozens of times with Angus MacKenzie about the woolen mills, and I can assure you that the last thing that will kill him is apoplexy."

Callie looked insulted. "Your father and Papa did leave Mr. MacKenzie in charge of the woolen mills with specific instructions that you and Dee were to be responsible for them someday. If Dee goes to Philadelphia, he's certainly not going to run the mills from there."

"Don't be upset," James said with a smile. "I've talked at length with Mr. MacKenzie, and I know he'll follow your father's instructions down to the last comma. He told me he's planning to train Dee in the business just as soon as Dee wants to come to Scotland. Don't worry about it."

"But if he goes off to explore the frontier . . ."

James reached out and took her hand. "Callie, that isn't going to happen. I'll talk to him. I'm sure I can persuade him."

"There's more." Her voice was small.

James waited, still holding to her hand. "Go on," he finally prompted.

"I'm afraid Dee's been gambling," Callie said. "I don't know for certain, but I think he has."

James stifled a smile. "Doesn't everyone?" He patted her hand. "Don't worry about it. All boys want to try horse racing, boxing, and gambling as well as, uh, other pursuits. I'll talk to him about it, but I'm sure it's nothing. As I recall, Dee is much like your father, so I'm sure he's a fine boy."

Percy sipped at his tea and stared out the window. "It's almost stopped raining, James," he said, louder than necessary.

James blinked and looked at him, but said nothing. "James," Percy said, putting his tea down, "don't you want to get out and walk around? I thought you had a pressing appointment."

"Appointment?" James said blankly. "I didn't . . ."

"You didn't remember?" Percy interrupted. "How very like you." He turned to Callie. "I don't know what James would do without me around to keep him on top of things."

"You?" James looked at Percy indignantly. "You can't keep up with your own hat, Percy. *I'm* the one who has to keep reminding you of your responsibilities."

"You? Responsible?" Callie's dimples deepened as she tried not to smile. Finally she gave up and laughed. "Jamie, please remember that I've known you forever." She gathered up the tea things. "If you need to go somewhere, you don't have to try to pretend I'm some green girl. I recognize a contrived excuse when I hear it."

"But I wasn't . . ."

"You're looking just the way you did the time you tried to get rid of me so you and Robin Miller could slip off to the village to see the Torrance twins."

"You *knew* about that?" James grinned at her. "I should have known—I never could get away with anything when you were around."

"Which is why I've always liked you so much," Callie said with a laugh, "and why your father always liked to have me around."

"But you never told on me," James said, "or at least, not very often."

40

"Not as much as I should have," Callie said. "But go on to wherever you're going. Aunt Mary will be expecting you for dinner, of course."

"Wonderful," Percy said.

"Aunt Mary hasn't seen Percy's appetite," James said with a chuckle. "She may chase us away when she sees how much he eats."

"Never. By the way, does your 'appointment' take you toward Gay Street or Cheap Street? I need to go out myself, especially since I've been cooped in the house for days with this rain. I might walk with you part of the way."

"Gay Street?" Percy feigned surprise. "Isn't that where you said Miss Bramley lives?"

Callie nodded. "I need to buy some supplies and then I think I'll check on Venetia. She's, uh, somewhat under the weather."

"She looked fine to me," James said.

"A cold. I just wanted to make sure she got home without a chill." Callie's face turned pink.

James gave her a strange look, then a smile. "We were going in that general direction, and we'd be delighted to escort you." Callie called for her pelisse and he helped her into it.

They walked along the walks, deftly avoiding puddles. The rainwater was still running along the streets. "Are you going to the library or the mantua maker's?" James asked as they walked. "Or perhaps just out to buy a bit of ribbon?"

"Oh, no. I'm buying some supplies for my work, then I plan to stop by Venetia's and see how she is." Callie rushed before Jamie could ask more. "I also promised to help her select a dress for her portrait."

41

James heard only one word and his jaw dropped in surprise. "Work?" he croaked. "Work? Whatever are you saying, Callie? You don't have to work. Lord knows, you've got a fortune of your own."

"I know that, you goose," Callie said, taking his arm. "But you should know me well enough to know that I'm not going to stay indoors the rest of my life doing needlework." She smiled up at him. "I wanted to *do* something."

"Work." James repeated the word. "Callie, women don't just *work*—that is, unless they have to. If you wanted to do something, why couldn't you take up good works or some such?" He paused. "By the way, just what do you do?"

Callie looked up at him and gave him her dimpled smile. "I paint portraits."

"Portraits?" There was a silence. "Good Lord, Callie, Pettigrew told me you painted, but do you mean you get out and do these things for . . ." he took a breath, "for *money?*"

Callie smiled and nodded. "As you said, I don't need the money, but for some reason, getting paid for my work makes it seem . . ."

"Makes it seem as if I'm turning you into a pauper."

"Don't be ridiculous, Jamie. Getting paid for my portraits makes me feel more like a real painter."

James put his hand to his head. "Callie, I'm your guardian. Do you know how this looks?"

"Bosh. Why would anyone in the *ton* care at all about Miss Callista Stone, daughter of Matthew Stone, a man whose wealth came from woolen mills? You know how the *ton* is—if you can't trace your lineage back to William the Conqueror, you don't count."

"Hardly," James said, "and for some, money counts more than blood. I hate to think what my father would say."

"Your father knew," Callie told him. "As a matter of fact, he encouraged me to paint." She paused at the corner. "I need to go into Cheap Street to purchase some canvas. This way." Percy and James turned with her. "You know how your father prized his Gainsboroughs, and he told me my portraits were well on the way to being as good as those." She smiled. "Of course, I knew it was flattery, but it was encouraging. Your father had a good eye for paintings, and he was the first to notice the similarity between my style and Gainsborough's."

Percy cleared his throat. "I believe Gainsborough lived in Bath at one time, didn't he?"

Callie nodded. "Yes. Here we are. Do you want to go in with me, or do you prefer to wait? I won't be a moment."

"I'll wait," James said, still dazed. He watched Callie make her way into the shop and thread through assorted canvases and shelves of paints. "I don't believe it, Percy," he said. "The problem with Dee is nothing—Callie's the problem. Portraits, indeed."

"I'm sure they're very good," Percy said.

"Oh, I have no doubt of it. Whatever Callie does, she does well. But *work*—getting *paid* for painting. This is one problem I'm going to have to solve." He paused and grimaced. "And before anyone finds out about it."

"You mean this is another problem," corrected

Percy. "There's also the problem of you getting leg-shackled."

"That's no problem, I assure you." He glanced at the door with a soft smile. "That hit me like a lightning bolt, Percy. Everytime I see her I hear those bells again."

"I told you," Percy said with finality, "that was just the beginning of a cold in your ears."

James laughed. "Then I think this is one cold I'm going to have trouble getting rid of. Right now I don't mind it at all."

Percy thought about the scene in the entryway. "It takes two, you know. I'm not sure anyone except you is hearing those bells."

James laughed. "Maybe not right now, but wait — I'm going to make sure she hears them too."

"This I've got to see," Percy said as the two of them settled down to wait for Callie. "Maybe you'll need my help after all."

"Absolutely not — I'm going this one alone," James said with a grin. He leaned against the side of the building and changed the topic of conversation to the latest race run by Lord Bamborough. The *on-dit* was that the young rakehell had overturned his carriage and commandeered a mail coach.

Chapter Three

Callie came out of the shop carrying an unwieldy parcel which James took from her. "Now where?" he asked. "Are you going to Miss Bramley's next?"

Callie looked at her parcel. "I was, but now . . ." She paused. "I'd really like to get right to work preparing this canvas.

"Ain't Miss Bramley expecting you?" Percy asked, giving James a small nudge with his elbow.

"Yes, I told her I'd stop by, but I don't know . . . perhaps I should take this home and see Venetia later this afternoon . . . or tomorrow."

"Oh, no need for that . . . I'll be glad to carry your parcel to Miss Bramley's and then home for you." James hoisted the package up on one shoulder and offered Callie his arm. The canvas was surprisingly heavy.

"What about your meeting?" Callie asked. "Didn't you have an urgent appointment this afternoon?"

"A misunderstanding—that was Percy," James answered promptly. "Do you need to go on now, Percy, or would you have time to go with us to Miss Bramley's?"

Percy stuttered and made a show of consulting his watch. "I believe I have the time to go with you if we don't stay long."

They walked slowly toward Gay Street, James shifting the package several times as he quizzed Callie about her life since they had last talked at length. The conversation veered off into their childhoods and some of the scrapes they gone through together. "You were altogether a hoyden, as I recollect," James said with a laugh as they rounded the corner into Gay Street.

"Hardly," Callie answered, laughing. "I was really quite prim and proper—and you were the rascal who was always leading me astray." She gestured to a house midway down the street. "There's Venetia's house."

"Rascal, indeed," James said indignantly. "I plan to argue the point with you later on." They strolled on down Gay Street, laughing, and stopped in front of the Bramley house. "Where did you meet Miss Bramley? I didn't know you were acquaintances."

"Oh, yes. I suppose you could say we're bosom bows. We first met at Madame Alexander's School. I was older, but we arrived on the same day." She laughed, remembering. "Venetia was such a skinny girl then. There was nothing to be seen but two big blue eyes."

"Very fine eyes," Percy said with enthusiasm.

"Uuummm," James agreed, shifting the canvas again. It seemed to be getting heavier and heavier.

"At any rate," Callie continued, "we kept in touch after we left school, and we visit regularly. She's in Bath now, with her family, so I don't get to see her as much as usual. She usually spends her time in Bath with Aunt Mary and me."

"I suppose your aunt wouldn't allow her to do otherwise," Percy said dryly.

Callie laughed. "Few people have opposed Aunt Mary and lived to tell the tale." She turned to James. "I don't want to impose on you any more than I have. Thank you for carrying my parcel. I shan't detain you any longer. I'll get one of the servants to carry this back home."

"Wonderful idea," Percy said, consulting his watch again. "James, we'd better be on our way."

"You'd better be on your way," James corrected. "I'll stay with Callie and walk her back home."

"I know you have other things to do, Jamie," Callie said, taking the package. "Besides, Venetia and I have some private matters to discuss, and I don't want to bore you by having you wait for me. I'll have one of her servants escort me home." With that she was up the steps, lifting the knocker. "I'll see the two of you at dinner. Good-bye, and thank you," she said cheerfully as she disappeared inside, leaving them standing on the paving stones, staring at each other.

Inside the house on Gay Street, Callie gave her parcel to a servant and was directed upstairs, where she found Venetia writing a letter. There were crumpled sheets littering the table and bits and pieces of torn paper on the floor. Venetia looked up as Callie came in, her eyes full of tears. "Oh, Callie, I'm so glad you're here!" she wailed, running across the room and embracing her.

"I wanted to see if you were feeling any better." Callie patted her shoulder. "Really, Venetia, every time I've seen you lately, you've been a watering pot. I thought love was supposed to be

47

a pleasant experience."

"It is, truly." Venetia wiped her eyes and sat down. "Almost always, anyway. I need you to help me compose a letter to Andrew."

"Weren't you planning to see him this afternoon?" Callie asked. "One of the reasons I wanted to visit was to try to stop you. Your reputation will be in shreds if anyone finds out."

Venetia's eyes filled again. "There's no need to stop me, Callie. I got a note from Andrew telling me absolutely not to come see him. He said we should abide by Papa's wishes for now, and that perhaps later we can convince Papa to allow us to marry."

"A sensible man," Callie answered, glancing at the tear-splashed note Venetia had handed her. "I think Captain Sinclair is right."

"He may be right, Callie, but it isn't what I want." She glanced at Callie. "And don't tell me that I'm spoiled, either. I already know that."

Callie laughed, a full, rich sound that brought a wavering grin to Venetia's face. "I won't tell you again, I promise." She put the letter on the table and leaned back in her chair. "So there's really no use to write Captain Sinclair, is there?"

Venetia shook her head in disagreement. "Not about seeing me this afternoon, but I have another plan . . . I want to write him and ask him to meet me at the Assembly Rooms tonight." She looked speculatively at Callie. "I need your help."

"Love letters aren't my forte, I'm afraid."

"You don't have to write anything, Callie. I want you to help me by pretending to have Andrew as an escort this evening."

48

Callie shook her head. "Your father would know better than that. No gentleman offers for one lady in the morning and escorts another that evening."

"I've thought of that," Venetia said gleefully. "I told Papa that you were Andrew's real love, and he was only offering for me on the rebound because you had told Andrew that the two of you could only be friends."

"Good Lord, Venetia, your scheming is going to get all of us in the suds. That's an out-and-out lie."

"A fib, and I wouldn't have told it if it hadn't been absolutely necessary." Venetia came over and sat beside her, taking her hand. "Please, Callie, let Andrew escort you to the Assembly Rooms. There'll be such a crush there that no one will notice. Papa will think he's with you and I'll be able to slip away and talk to him."

"Venetia, the captain doesn't need to escort me. He can go by himself. I'd serve no purpose."

"Yes, you would. Papa would think Andrew had given up trying to make you jealous by offering for me and had fixed his attention on you again. I could flirt outrageously with someone else, and then, when the time was right, Andrew and I could talk." She looked at her friend pleadingly. "Please, Callie, please."

Callie sighed. "It's a completely harebrained scheme, Venetia. Still . . ." She paused and gave up. "How have you always been able to talk all of us into doing what you wished, even when we knew it was wrong? At school you even managed to convince that poor Miss Applebury to do whatever you wanted."

"That wasn't easy, I assure you." A mischievous grin flitted across Venetia's face. "Will you do this for me,

Callie? I need to speak to Andrew, and I promise I won't ask you again."

"All right—just this once. I don't intend to be part of anything that goes against your father's wishes." Callie attempted to look stern. "I want you to know that I really don't feel at all the thing doing this."

Venetia hugged her. "Just this once. If I can only speak to Andrew, I promise I'll do what Papa asks of me. Truly."

Venetia turned and scribbled a few lines on a sheet of foolscap, then rang for her maid. "There," she said as she sealed and sanded the letter. "I've told Andrew to come by and escort you to the Rooms. How lucky you are!"

Callie gave her friend a skeptical glance. "That remains to be seen. However am I going to explain this to Aunt Mary?"

"I'm sure you'll think of something. You always do."

"Am I to understand that Captain Sinclair has suddenly felt the need for your company?" Aunt Mary fixed Callie with a sharp look.

"Not exactly, Aunt Mary." Callie searched for a reasonable explanation. "It seems that Venetia has decided that the captain was much too serious, and he merely wishes to talk to me about the situation. He certainly hasn't fixed his attentions on me." She stared hard at a print behind Aunt Mary's head as she spoke and fully expected lightening bolts to strike at any moment. Aunt Mary didn't seem to notice her fabrications for what they were.

"He should fix his attentions on you, I think," her

aunt said bluntly. "You're a much better prospect than Venetia—the poor girl has absolutely no sense at all." Aunt Mary gave her a critical glance and Callie felt herself go pale. "If the captain wants to talk about Venetia, why doesn't he speak to her directly?" Aunt Mary asked practically.

"He has, but you know how these things are," Callie said vaguely, backing away toward the door so she could beat a retreat.

"Things were different in my day." Aunt Mary sniffed. "I simply don't know what's happening to the younger generation." She pinned Callie with a glance. I don't know about his prospects, but I do approve of the captain taking you—he cuts a fine figure in that uniform, and who knows what may happen once he has the opportunity to talk with an intelligent woman?" She gave Callie a significant look. "Hadn't you best get ready if you're going?"

Callie fled in relief, Aunt Mary's voice following her up the stairs. "Be sure to wear your best striped dress and your cashmere."

Callie paused only long enough to answer "yes" and dashed on up the stairs, counting herself lucky to have escaped more questions. On the landing she met Percy. "How was your appointment?" she asked.

"Appointment? Appointment? Oh, couldn't have gone better." He reddened.

"Wonderful." Callie slipped past him. "Has Jamie had time to talk to Dee yet?"

Percy shook his head. "Not yet, but he's going to. I think he wants to talk to you further about Dee first. Don't want to jump in feet first, you know. That would probably just make the boy angry."

Callie sighed. "That Jamie. Is that just an excuse? I wonder if he will ever do what he says he's going to?"

"Of course he will—and he does," Percy said. "And no, I don't think waiting is an excuse. It sounds sensible to me. James has always been more responsible than anyone gave him credit for."

Callie lifted an eyebrow, then laughed. "Responsible? This is Jamie we're discussing, Percy . . . surely you can't mean it."

"Well, I think his father . . ." Percy broke off, embarrassed. "I don't want to tell tales out of school."

Callie was intrigued. "I don't think you are. Remember, I'm practically a member of Jamie's family."

"True." Percy paused.

"Well?" Callie prompted.

Percy squirmed under her gaze, and Callie felt distinctly like Aunt Mary. Finally he spoke. "He isn't irresponsible, he really isn't. I know it seems that way, but that's only on the surface."

"Do you mean he's changed?"

Percy reddened again. "Not changed so much. He's just the same as he's always been. Since you knew him when he was a child, you know that his father was always after him for being irresponsible. Old Lord Atwater even wrote it into his will that James couldn't have his fortune until he either married or turned thirty." Percy frowned. "All the while, I think James was just as irresponsible as he needed to be to annoy his father, and now he seems determined to annoy old Pettigrew and the trustees his father put over him. It's as if he's trying to prove himself a wastrel so they can justify their opinions of him." He stopped and looked at Callie. "That doesn't make sense, I know, and please don't let James know I said anything of the sort."

"I wouldn't say anything at all," Callie said with a small frown. "I didn't know there was anything in his father's will."

"Oh, yes, James has the title, but he can't inherit the fortune until he marries or turns thirty, whichever comes first. His father thought marriage would make him responsible, even told old Pettigrew that." Percy was incensed. "That's why James is in Bath," he added.

"Jamie's in Bath because of his father's will?"

Percy nodded, glancing up at a noise from James's room and missing Callie's look. "Looking for a wife, he is. Just any wife will do, you know. That's what the will says—a wife. It don't specify."

Callie gritted her teeth to keep from saying anything, while Percy went on as he watched for James. "I thought of several he might marry who wouldn't bother him at all, but nothing would do him but come to Bath and court Venetia Bramley. I've promised to give him all the help I can, but . . ." He broke off as James's door opened and he came out, glancing up and down the hall.

"There you are, Percy. Hello, Callie."

"Jamie." Callie's voice was ice, but James didn't notice.

James gave her his particularly charming smile. "How was your visit with Miss Bramley? You found her well, I hope?" He came to the top of the steps, dressed for the evening in a black coat, cream breeches, and a white waistcoat brocaded with unopened rosebuds. Angry as she was, Callie had to admit that he looked splendid. She forced herself to glare at him. "Fine," she said shortly. "I understand you haven't talked to Dee yet."

James shook his head. "No, but I plan to just . . ."

"It certainly seems as if you could do that one small thing, Jamie," Callie snapped. "You've done precious little for him except send money now and then. Come to think of it, you didn't even do that—you had your secretary do it, I'm sure."

"Actually, Pettigrew took care of that," James said mildly. "As I was saying . . ."

"You didn't come to Bath because of him, did you? You didn't plan on speaking to him at all, did you?" Callie's voice shook with anger. "I've been so worried about him—he's been into gambling and carousing and heaven knows what else, and you don't even care. All the while I thought you had come here because you cared about Dee, and now you won't even speak to him."

James looked at her curiously. "I plan to speak to him at the first opportunity, Callie. Dee happens to be visiting his friends in Bristol and won't be back until tomorrow. Or at least that's what Aunt Mary tells me."

"Oh." Callie felt herself go red as she recalled that Dee had been gone since yesterday. "Well, I expect you to speak to him at the very first opportunity," she said, salvaging what she could. With a quick glare that included both James and Percy, she fled to her room.

In spite of Aunt Mary's instructions, Callie spent very little time on her appearance. After all, Captain Sinclair certainly didn't care about *her* dress. He would have eyes for no one except Venetia. Callie decided to wear her old sea green gown, but her maid, Brewster, like Aunt Mary, insisted on her striped muslin trimmed with ribbons. Brewster, over Callie's protests, even put her hair up in matching ribbons. Callie couldn't concentrate on her appearance — the more she thought about the scene on the steps, the angrier she became. She was fairly fuming at James when Captain Sinclair was announced and had to stop and remind herself that the Captain had no part in her anger and mortification. She forced herself to smile and be pleasant as she descended the stairs.

"You look lovely," Captain Sinclair said gallantly, handing her a small bouquet of violets done up in a purple ribbon.

Callie looked at him in some surprise, and then decided the speech had been made for Aunt Mary's benefit. Aunt Mary gave Captain Sinclair a critical appraisal, then smiled and nodded approvingly. Callie bowed her head to keep from laughing aloud at her aunt's expression. She thanked Captain Sinclair profusely and warmly just for Aunt Mary, then they set out for the Assembly Rooms.

"I hope this arrangement tonight hasn't inconvenienced you," Captain Sinclair said formally, once they were out of earshot. "I don't wish to disappoint Venetia, but I don't wish to intrigue against her father's wishes."

"Nor do I," Callie agreed.

"I told Venetia that I would meet her only this once." He paused. "I plan on going away, and then I can return for her."

"Business?" Callie asked, more out of politeness than interest.

The captain nodded. "I haven't said anything to

Miss Bramley or her father, but I plan to resign my commission. My uncle is Lord Easton, and he's promised to try to arrange a position for me. The prospects are excellent." He turned and looked at Callie. "Do you think she'll wait for me, Miss Stone?" His carefully controlled expression only made him look more anguished.

Callie patted him on the arm. "I'm sure she will, Captain Sinclair. Venetia cares for you very much."

He sighed with relief. "You've eased my mind considerably, Miss Stone," he said, taking her arm to escort her into the rooms.

Callie wished her own mind was eased considerably. As much as Venetia fancied herself in love, she was flighty enough forget the captain a week after he was out of her sight. Even worse, Callie was convinced that the captain was the perfect match for Venetia, except for his lack of fortune. He was also devoted to her. Callie glanced around, searching for her friend, and feeling completely ill at ease. All in all, she thought, the whole situation was a coil, and she had a vague presentiment that this scheme, like so many of the other schemes Venetia had concocted, was not going to go as planned.

She and Captain Sinclair saw Venetia at the same moment. Callie felt the captain go tense. Venetia was flirting outrageously with someone as her mother stood close, smiling. "I don't believe it," Captain Sinclair muttered under his breath.

At that moment, Venetia's companion turned, and it was Callie's turn to gasp. Venetia was flirting with — of all people — James.

"It's only a pretense," Callie murmured to the captain. "That's Viscount Atwater. Jamie's almost . . . he's like family. Venetia is only being congenial for her father's benefit. See? Her father's watching her." She nudged the captain's attention to where Venetia's father, Sir Dudley, was watching Venetia flirt with James. Sir Dudley was beaming and keeping Percy occupied with his war stories.

Captain Sinclair forced himself to look away from Venetia and down at Callie. "Thank you," he said with a smile. "Perhaps we need to keep up our part of the pretense. I suggest we visit with some other guests." With that, he tucked her hand under his arm and gently propelled her into step beside a group of rather elderly ladies heading for the refreshments. The crush was such that it took the two of them the better part of half an hour to work their way around to where James and Venetia were standing.

Venetia glimpsed them first. "My goodness, Viscount Atwater," she said in mock surprise. "Look who's here."

James turned and Callie found herself staring right up at him. All her chagrin of the afternoon returned. He brought up his quizzing glass and looked from Callie to Captain Sinclair while Venetia made the introductions.

"Delighted," James said, in a voice that did not seem delighted at all.

Captain Sinclair nodded absently. He was unable to stop staring at Venetia, who was, Callie admitted to herself, quite fetching in a pink-and-white striped silk twill. They stood in silence for a moment, then Venetia gave Callie a sharp nudge in the ribs.

"Oh!" Callie gasped, catching her breath in surprise, then picked up her cue. "Jamie," she asked, gritting her teeth and forcing the words out, "would you please escort me over to get something to drink?" She made herself smile broadly at him. Venetia would never know of this sacrifice. "It's really hot in here. I do believe I could use a glass of water."

James looked at her, puzzled. "Callie, you're carrying a cup of tea."

Callie looked down at the forgotten tea in her hand. "It's really become rather hot in this crush," she said, groping for words, "and then I do feel quite faint." She put her hand on her forehead. "Really, Jamie, I do need some fresh tea."

"I'll be glad to get it for you," Percy said. "I could use some myself." Before Callie could protest, he was off toward the refreshment tables. Venetia nudged Callie again in the ribs, but before she could think of anything else to say, Sir Dudley gave them his full attention.

"Ah, Captain Sinclair," he said approvingly, noting Callie standing with her hand placed on the captain's arm, "delighted to see you. I was just telling these gentlemen about the atrocities I witnessed at Valmy in '92. Tell me, have you seen for yourself any of the massacres that have been attributed to Napoleon?" With an expertise Callie had never dreamed of, Sir Dudley stepped between Captain Sinclair and Venetia and quite effectively managed to move both Callie and the captain well away from James and Venetia. Percy returned with a cup of tea and monopolized Callie, while Sir Dudley monopolized Captain Sinclair for the rest of the evening. Every now and then Callie caught an imploring glance from Venetia, but she was powerless. Finally, after some loud and blatant hints from Sir Dudley, James offered to escort Venetia and her mother home. After the three of them had left, Sir Dudley took his leave of Callie and Captain Sinclair with a self-satisfied smile. He then moved on to other prey who hadn't yet heard the stories of his battle prowess.

"Quite an impossible evening," Captain Sinclair said, giving Callie a glance.

"Oh, I rather enjoyed the stories," Percy said, draining yet another cup of tea. "Callie, do you mind if I go home with you and the captain? James has left me high and dry here." He chuckled. "I've got fifty pounds riding on this thing, and it looks as if I'm going to lose it, but I don't mind. A good cause, you know."

"Fifty pounds on what?" Callie asked.

"On James marrying Venetia Bramley," Percy said, turning to look for a place to put down his cup. "Don't you remember? I told you about it this afternoon." Captain Sinclair started so violently that Callie pulled on his arm and squeezed his fingers to quiet him.

"What did you say?" she asked Percy as he turned back to them.

"I told you James wanted to marry Venetia Bramley."

"Venetia?"

"Yes, she's the one, all right." He sounded exasperated.

There was a stunned silence, then Callie spoke. "What's this about fifty pounds?" Callie was still hanging onto Captain Sinclair's fingers, and felt as if her smile were frozen in place for eternity.

"Oh, that . . . yes, I put fifty pounds on it. I bet

James that he couldn't do it — marry Venetia Bramley, I mean — but he said it was a sure thing. Said love had hit him like a lightening bolt, can you believe that?"

"No." Callie's voice was like ice.

"It's true. He's even hearing wedding bells," Percy said, oblivious to both Callie and Captain Sinclair. "I should have believed him, shouldn't I? I suppose it'll cost me fifty pounds, but confidentially, it'll cost Jamie more than that in the long run." He turned back around and picked up his empty teacup. "Are you ready to leave now? If you aren't, I believe I'll have some more tea, although in all honesty, this stuff shouldn't properly be called tea."

"Leave now?" Captain Sinclair said in a strangled voice. "I think . . . I think . . ." His voice broke a little and he was unable to continue.

"Now. Let's go home now." Callie shoved the captain unceremoniously in front of her. "It's late, and I need to get up to catch the early light for a painting."

"Capital!" Percy said, looking into the depths of his teacup. "This dratted stuff was getting a little wearing. I could use something a little stronger."

"Couldn't we all?" Callie sighed as she gave Captain Sinclair another shove toward the door.

Chapter Four

Callie shut the door behind her and sagged against it. Percy looked at her curiously. It had been a terrible trip home—Captain Sinclair had been too shocked to speak for the first few minutes, but that, of course, was before he got angry.

"I won't have it!" he had exclaimed in the silence, causing both Callie and Percy to jump. "I won't be made a fool of!" He had crashed his fist against his thigh with a thud.

"It's nothing, I assure you," Callie had said quickly, trying to give Captain Sinclair a look to warn him not to speak in front of Percy. Unfortunately, in the dark, the captain couldn't see a thing, so he kept right on ranting. "I'll call him out, that's what I'll do! The nerve of that London jack-a-napes! Who does he think he is? What does he think he's doing? I'll . . . I'll . . ." He finally stopped, sputtering for words.

Callie had no choice "Please, Captain Sinclair, not here. Please. This is a private matter." This last was said with a glance at Percy, which again the captain failed to see.

"Damn right it's a private matter," the captain

growled. "Pardon me, Miss Stone, but I intend . . ."

"Oh, I intend to do the same," Callie interrupted, seeing a mental image of herself breaking Venetia's neck at the first opportunity, "but I assure you that this . . . this *affair* isn't what it seems. If you will come see me tomorrow, I'm sure everything can be explained. I'm sure you'll understand when everyone is there. *Everyone.*" There was a pause. "Please believe me. As I told you, Jamie's almost like family to me."

Captain Sinclair took a deep breath to control himself. He evidently had not missed Callie's emphasis on *everyone.* "Very well, Miss Stone. I'll call on you as early as is convenient." They stopped in front of his lodgings, and the light from the torches fell full on his face. He reached over and touched Callie's hand. "Are we agreed, then?"

Callie nodded and smiled in reassurance, her fingers clasping the captain's. "We are agreed, Captain, though perhaps early afternoon . . ." She paused, wondering how she could possibly get Venetia out early enough to meet with the captain.

"I hate to wait, but . . . done. I'll plan to see you, and your friend." Captain Sinclair smiled briefly and left them.

Callie looked at Percy and was horrified to see an amazed expression on his face. "This isn't what it seems," she stammered.

"You and Captain Sinclair? Was he jealous of James, and thought you and James . . . ? Lud, I didn't know the wind blew that way, or I'd have come on later."

"Percy, really, you've misunderstood. The captain and I are merely friends. Acquaintances, actually."

He chuckled and patted her hand. "Don't worry, your secret is safe with me." He chuckled again. "Maybe we'll have two weddings at once. Does your Aunt Mary know?"

"There's nothing to know. Percy, I'm telling you . . ." she began, but it was no use. No matter what she said, he believed she was carrying on with Andrew Sinclair, and even worse, believed she was doing such a thing in secret. By the time they reached Pulteney Street, Callie's nerves were a frayed mess.

"I need tea," she muttered to the maid, as she went toward the parlor. "Strong tea. And hurry."

"I was hoping for something a little more powerful," Percy said, following her into the room. "That dratted tea was foul stuff."

"You're right, Percy. This calls for something stronger." She reached for the sherry and poured each of them a large glassful.

Percy looked at the amount and then at Callie. "Drink up," she said, downing hers in gulps.

Three glasses of sherry later, the tea was brought in. Callie motioned to Margaret, the downstairs maid, to put it on the table and then dismissed her. "Help yourself, Percy," she said, pouring herself another glass of sherry. "What's this? It's all gone." She went to the cupboard and fetched another decanter. "This will do." She finished filling her glass.

"Perhaps you should have tea instead of sherry and whatever that is. You're not accustomed to drinking much, are you?" Percy looked at her doubtfully.

"No, I seldom drink anything, but I assure you, Percy, I feel fine. Very fine, indeed. Actually, I have a clear head." She drank the contents of her glass down in one swallow and choked. Percy beat her on the back until she finally stopped coughing and caught her breath. "Heavens, that was strong," she gasped, wiping tears from her eyes.

Percy picked it up and tasted it. "Good Lord! That's whiskey."

"Impossible, Aunt Mary would never allow whiskey."

"That's what I'm afraid of."

They were interrupted by a noise from the outside door and Percy hid the cut-glass bottle behind a cushion. In a few moments, the parlor door opened. "What's this? A late-night party?" James strolled in and looked from one to the other.

Callie reached under the cushion, retrieved the bottle, and refilled her glass. "A party," she repeated, raising the glass in salute before she drank most of it. "Lovely party." She giggled.

Percy looked at James with a stricken expression. "Wasn't my fault. Really."

James reached over and took the glass from Callie, sniffed it, then tasted the liquid. "Whiskey? Good God, Callie, you're drinking whiskey?"

"Of course not," she said with a giggle. "Sherry. You know Aunt Mary wouldn't allow whiskey in the house. Sherry. That's what. Good, strong sherry." She reached for the glass, but James held it out of her reach.

"No more, my girl," he said, putting both glass and decanter in the cupboard. He looked at Percy. "What brought this on?"

"It really wasn't my fault."

"I know that. I know Callie well enough from years

past to understand that when she decides to do something, few people can stop her. She's like a headstrong horse."

Callie was insulted. "Really, Jamie. A horse. I've never been called a horse in my life." She put a hand to her head to see if that would make the room steady. It was beginning to spin around. "A horse. Oh, Jamie, how could you?" A tear slid down her cheek.

James sighed and mopped at her face with his handkerchief. "Here, now." He handed her the damp handkerchief and sat her down on the sofa. "I'll deal with you later, my girl," James said. He gave Percy a stern glance. "Now, what brought this on?"

"Some sort of row she and Captain Sinclair had. It seems they have a . . . um, an understanding, and something went awry. I believe he was jealous of you, or some such. At any rate, they're supposed to meet tomorrow morning to straighten it out. They was both up in the boughs about whatever it was." He glanced at Callie. "If you think she's in a state, you should have heard *him*."

"Captain Sinclair." James turned to Callie as he said the name slowly. "I had no idea." He regarded Callie with a strange, speculative look.

"Not what you think," she mumbled. "Not what you think *at all*." She began humming and trying to fit the words into a song, swaying from side to side.

"Good Lord, Callie, you're drunk!" James came over, stood over her, and tilted her face up so he could see it.

"No, oh, noooo. Never," she crooned. "Drunk, drink. 'Drink to me only with thine eyes / And I will pledge with mine.'" She tried to stand, but swayed as the room seemed to begin spinning again. She sagged heavily against James. " 'Or leave a kiss but in the cup,' " she sang, and looked up into his brown eyes. Her knees buckled, and she felt dizzy, swimming in the spell of his warm brown eyes. "Kiss, kiss in the cup," she crooned, putting her head on his chest. It felt so *right*, so comfortable. She sighed deeply. "Sleep, Jamie, sleep."

" 'Sleep' is right, my girl," he said, catching her as she slid downward. "How on earth are we going to get you upstairs and into bed without waking up the entire household?"

"Kiss, kiss, Jamie," Callie crooned, oblivious to what he was saying. "Need to sleep."

James pulled her up and caught her around the waist to keep her upright. "Percy," he ordered, "look outside and see if anyone's in the hall. Maybe we can get her upstairs."

Percy peered around the door. "All clear."

James picked up Callie. She put her arms around his neck and nestled against him. "Jamie," she mumbled.

"Hush, girl," he whispered against her hair as he followed Percy out the door and carried her up the stairs. She ignored him and kept humming, while she entwined the curls at his neck through her fingers. "For God's sake, Callie, stop that," he whispered hoarsely, trying to turn his head. It did no good.

Callie's room was at the end of the hall, just past Aunt Mary's room. Just as James got in front of his door, Percy made a strangled sound and pointed toward Aunt Mary's door, which was slowly opening and casting a square of light into the hall. Quickly,

James opened his own door and dumped Callie unceremoniously on the floor. "Sleep," she mumbled, stretching out as he closed the door.

"I thought I heard something," Aunt Mary said, coming out into the hall in her dressing gown. "I had forgotten the hours young men keep. In my day, young men were in early and out early to hunt. Nothing like today, when you young people stay up all night."

"I'm sorry we disturbed you," James said, as there was a small thump from the other side of the door.

"What was that?" Aunt Mary asked, frowning at the door.

"What?" James's face was the picture of innocence.

"That noise. I thought I heard something."

"Noise? I didn't hear anything. Did you, Percy?"

Percy shook his head vigorously as James pretended to trip and fall against the door to cover the sound of another thump. "I don't mean to be unmannerly," James said, but it's much past my bedtime. I'm not quite used to these late hours."

"Good," Aunt Mary said approvingly. She glanced down the hall. "Perhaps I'd better check on Callie."

"Oh no," James said hastily. "She returned much earlier with Percy, so I imagine she's been asleep for a while now."

"You young people." Aunt Mary shook her head. "Good night."

James went into his room, shoving Percy ahead of him. Percy almost fell over Callie, who was sleeping soundly on the floor. "Lud, what a coil," Percy said. "What are you going to do now?"

James sat down in a chair and looked down at Callie. "*We* are going to wait for an hour or so until Aunt Mary goes back to sleep, and then we're going to get Callie to bed."

"How are we going to do that?" Percy asked. "It just ain't right to take someone like Miss Stone and put her to bed. It just ain't good *ton,* if you know what I mean."

"Good *ton* be damned right now," James said wearily. "We're going to take Callie into her room, dump her on the bed, and cover her up. She'll sleep all right just the way she is." He looked at Percy sharply. "What else can you tell me about Callie and Captain Sinclair? This just isn't like Callie."

Percy looked worried. "I don't suppose I'm talking out of turn. After all, as Callie said, you're family. It's just that she and Captain Sinclair seem to have some kind of understanding. All of this seems to be going on without her aunt's knowledge because she was worried about anyone knowing. Kept talking nonsense about how things seemed to be. Very secretive, I thought, which is why I didn't know exactly what had happened. Callie kept telling him that his fears were groundless, or some such."

Callie rolled over on the floor and mumbled. "We can't leave her on the floor," James said. "Perhaps we should put her on the bed." He bent down and scooped her up from the floor.

"On *your* bed!" Percy was horrified. "James, it just ain't the thing, I'm telling you."

James held Callie in his arms and regarded Percy coolly. "And I suppose it is the thing to leave her on the floor and have to step over her for the next half hour? Besides, it's damned uncomfortable and cold down there—I know from experience. Now move."

Percy got up and backed up against the door while James placed Callie carefully in the middle of the bed and put pillows on one side of her so she wouldn't roll off. He sat back down in the chair and looked at Percy. "You might as well sit down, too. We'll have to give Aunt Mary at *least* a half hour more before we dare try to carry Callie to her room."

"Maybe we should wait an hour before we try it." Percy sat down in a straight chair across from James and looked nervously at the door as they sat in silence for what seemed like hours.

Finally James spoke. "Back to Captain Sinclair." He frowned as he glanced over at the sleeping girl on the bed. "This isn't like Callie at all—not unless she's changed drastically since . . . since we were younger." He looked back at Percy. "So you think they've been meeting clandestinely?"

"It sounded that way to me." He looked troubled. "It may not be like her, but you know how unpredictable women are. I thought she and Captain Sinclair were quite besotted with each other."

James stood and looked down at Callie's sleeping form. He looked at her for a long time, reaching over to lift a stray lock of hair from her face and put it back into place. "Callie," he said softly, almost to himself, "if he's really what you want, I won't say anything."

He turned and looked at Percy. "Check the hall. If it's clear, I'll carry her to her room. We'll have to leave word for her dresser that she's ill. The last thing she's going to need in the morning will be someone barging in to wake her up early." He smiled. "I imagine Callie will be feeling the effects of this for most of the day tomorrow." He lifted her up easily, and she snuggled against him with a mumble and put her arms around his neck.

Percy peered out and motioned James out into the hall. They went quietly by Aunt Mary's room, but Percy rattled the knob of Callie's door loudly before he got it open. As soon as James was inside, he motioned for Percy to close the door quickly while he put Callie carefully on the bed. "Let's hurry and get out of here," he said. "Every minute we're here increases our risk of being discovered." He slipped off Callie's shoes and covered her up carefully. She woke for a moment, looked up at him, and smiled. "Jamie," she mumbled, holding out her hand.

He clasped her fingers and tucked them under the quilt. "Go to sleep," he said. She smiled sleepily at him again and closed her eyes. James looked from her to Percy. "Let's go. *Hurry.*"

Just as they touched the door, it was flung open, almost knocking Percy to the floor. He yelped, and James clapped a hand over his mouth to stifle the sound. Percy regained his feet, then they looked in the doorway.

Outside stood a very enraged young stripling, barefooted and in his nightshirt, carrying a large pistol. "Just who are you and what are you doing in my sister's room at this hour?" His voice was shaking with rage while the pistol waved from James to Percy and back again.

"Be quiet!" James hissed, looking at Aunt Mary's door.

"Why? Are you afraid of being caught and turned over to the magistrates?" The pistol shook as the young man pointed it at first one and then the other.

James reached out a hand, then drew back as the pistol barrel was pointed right at his chest. "Please be quiet," he said evenly. He noted the boy's curling auburn hair and dark blue eyes, so like Callie's. "You must be Dee," he said, very quietly. "Take a moment to think of Callie's reputation. What would it do to her if we were caught here?"

Dee nodded and wavered, looking across James's shoulder to Callie's bed. She was sleeping peacefully. He started to walk into the room, the pistol still pointed at James.

"No." James shook his head. "If you want to sort this out, let's go to my room. We don't dare be seen here." There was a pause as James glanced significantly toward Aunt Mary's door. "Quick, man. We've got to leave."

Dee hesitated and motioned James and Percy by him. "My room. There." He pointed with the pistol barrel and the two edged by him and into the room adjoining Callie's. Dee followed them and closed the door behind him. "Now, just who are you, and why are you here?"

James sat down on the edge of the bed. "I wish you'd put that pistol away," he said irritably. "You're going to blow someone's head off." He made the introductions. "I'm James Williford, Viscount Atwater, your guardian, I believe, since I assume you're De-Quincey Stone, back early from Bristol. This other gentleman is my friend Percy Golightly."

Dee heard only the first name. "My guardian. I suppose you've answered Callie's summons and come to show me the error of my ways."

71

James smiled. "Not really," he said truthfully. "Are your ways in error? I did hear something about you being sent down from school and wanting to emigrate, but that was all."

"I'm going, and you're not going to stop me."

James looked at him coolly. "Far be it from me to stop you. I do, however, wish you'd put away that pistol. I assure you that neither of us is dangerous."

Dee looked down at the pistol in his hand as if he didn't recognize it. "It isn't loaded," he said, putting it in a drawer.

There was a knock at the door. "DeQuincey? DeQuincey, are you awake? I thought I heard voices."

"Oh, Lord," Percy moaned. "We're in for it now."

"Quick, Percy. Under the bed." James gave him a shove.

"But . . ."

"Don't argue, get under there."

Percy rolled under the bed, and James grabbed Dee and shoved him toward the bed. "Quick, get in." Without a word, Dee crawled in. James jerked off his coat and waistcoat, stuffing them under the bed with Percy. As he walked across the room he untied his cravat and let the ends dangle. Then he opened the door. "Aunt Mary, I'm sorry if we woke you," he said suavely, blocking the door. "After I began getting ready for bed, I heard Dee in the hall, and we were just getting acquainted. It had been such a long time since we'd seen each other that we hated to wait until morning."

Aunt Mary peered around him and looked into the room. "I thought I heard voices — several voices," she said disapprovingly. "In my day, people went to bed at a decent hour."

"I'm sorry, I truly am," James said to her with his most charming smile. "I hadn't seen DeQuincey since he was much younger, and I couldn't wait to talk to him. We certainly didn't mean to disturb you."

"It's fine, Aunt Mary," Dee said from the bed. "I was so excited about talking to . . ." He groped for a name. . . . to . . ."

"I told you to forget titles and just call me James," James said smoothly.

"I'll try to remember that," Dee said. "I got so excited about talking to James that I invited him to come in and get acquainted."

Aunt Mary sniffed. "I suggest the both of you get to sleep. At least that's what *I* intend to do. For the third time."

"Yes, Aunt Mary," James and Dee said together as she marched across the hall and into her room. James closed the door behind her as Percy rolled out from under the bed, clutching James's clothes.

"Dratted dusty under there," he said, brushing himself off. "I was afraid I was going to sneeze. You'd better get after the maids."

"Aunt Mary would have a conniption if she knew it was dusty," Dee said. "But I, for one, ain't going to tell her."

James chuckled. "I can imagine that explanation now." He gave Percy a good imitation of Aunt Mary's glare. "And what, young man, were you doing under the bed in the middle of the night?"

"Trust me—I won't say a word either," Percy said hastily.

Dee sat up on the edge of his bed, letting his feet

73

dangle. "You didn't tell me what you were doing in Callie's room."

"Putting her to bed — on the top of the bed with all her clothes on," James answered. "Don't get up in the boughs. There's a perfectly good explanation."

There was a long pause. "Would you like to give it to me?" Dee finally asked.

James sighed. "Callie was drunk."

Dee looked incredulous and then laughed aloud. "That's ridiculous. Callie doesn't drink anything except a small glass of wine once in a while."

"I think that's precisely why she got drunk." James looked at Percy. "Do you want to tell Dee what happened?"

"Gladly." He looked at Dee. "It's easy to understand. First, there was Captain Sinclair, and their argument, and then Callie seemed all upset and said they'd sort it out tomorrow and they should meet and his fears were groundless, then she got home and started drinking sherry, and then there was the whiskey." Percy looked from one to the other. "That's all there was to it."

James looked at Dee. "You see, it's all perfectly clear." They grinned at each other, then James became serious. "Callie and Captain Sinclair have evidently been meeting without your aunt's knowledge. Do you know anything about it?"

"Andrew Sinclair?" Dee was puzzled. "Lord, that's news to me. I thought he was talking about marrying V . . . someone else." He looked from James to Percy. "Are you sure? Callie and Andrew Sinclair?"

"Positive," Percy answered promptly. "They're besotted with each other."

"I just can't believe it. They don't suit at all." Dee

74

stood and began pacing the room. "Besides, it ain't like Callie to go carrying on behind someone's back." He paced some more, dodging Percy. "They just don't suit," he said at last. "Callie's not a stiff-necked prig like Sinclair. Callie's. . . ." He paused, looking for the right word. "Callie's *fun*."

James lifted a quizzical eyebrow. "What did you say about the captain planning to marry someone else?"

Dee shrugged. "That was the last I heard from Callie. It could have been all a hum, I suppose, a smokescreen to cover what was going on between him and Callie." He stopped and shook his head. "It just don't fit—Callie and the captain, I mean."

"A smokescreen!" Percy frowned as he looked from Dee to James. "That must be it—Callie and Captain Sinclair have been very clever. Only a military mind could think of a scheme like that to hide a *tendre* from your Aunt Mary."

"But why would they want to hide it?" Dee asked, confused.

Percy shook his head. "Never question what a woman does, my boy. No one ever knows the reasons."

Dee shook his head. "It still don't ring right. Something doesn't fit here, I'd stake my allowance on it."

James gathered up his clothes and feigned a yawn. "Percy, we should take Aunt Mary's advice and go on to bed." He turned and put a hand on Dee's shoulder. "I'm of your opinion—something doesn't sound quite right. I hope you and I can put our heads together tomorrow and see if we can untangle this bramble." He chuckled. "I doubt if Callie will be in any condition to assist us, so I assume this is one we'll have to figure out for ourselves."

Chapter Five

Callie woke up the next morning with the sun in her eyes. It looked and felt as if fireworks were going off behind her eyeballs. She reached over and rang for Brewster, then groaned as the sound reverberated from one ear to the other.

"Good morning, Miss Stone," Brewster said cheerfully, slamming the door behind her. "The Viscount told me you were ill and not to bother you. I was worried right enough." Brewster sniffed. "As if I didn't know how to take care of a sick person."

"Please," Callie moaned, "just lay out some clothes and I'll dress myself."

"Well!" Brewster was offended. She put out a yellow-and-white striped muslin, slamming the cupboard doors as she did, and crashed Callie's yellow kid slippers down on the floor. "Will that be all?" she asked frigidly, insulted beyond words.

As soon as Brewster left, banging the door quite unnecessarily, Callie thought, Callie covered her eyes and allowed herself to groan again. She had never felt so horrible in her entire life and, as bits and pieces of the previous night fell into place in her memory, she had never felt so embarrassed. "I couldn't have," she muttered to herself as she tried to sit. She looked down and saw she was still wearing her striped dress. "I did," she said aloud, falling back against the pillows and covering her face against the astounding brightness of the sun.

It took her the better part of an hour to take off her clothes and get into the muslin. She felt *terrible,* and worse, when she forced herself to face the looking-glass, she looked, as Aunt Mary was fond of saying about others, like death warmed over.

Aunt Mary came in just as Callie had shoved her hair back, catching most of it in a yellow ribbon. "Atwater said you were not all the thing," she said anxiously, "and, my dear, you *do* look wretched. What you need is a good, hearty breakfast. Kidneys, perhaps."

Callie hung her head and fought down nausea and the thoughts of grilled kidneys. "I'm not hungry. Really."

"Nonsense." Aunt Mary flung open the curtains Callie had drawn to keep out the sun. "When you're ill, the best thing you can do is eat a good, substantial breakfast. If you convince yourself you're weak and sickly, then you will be." She took Callie's arm. "Come along, dear. Kidneys, eggs, muffins, and jam for you."

Callie shut her mouth firmly and forced herself to walk. Aunt Mary fancied herself an expert in caring for the sick; furthermore, when Aunt Mary commanded, there was nothing for it but to go.

Downstairs, Aunt Mary shoved her gently toward the parlor and went off to see about the household, warning that she would be in to see if Callie had eaten a good breakfast. Callie stammered out a "Yes, Aunt Mary" while trying to keep from casting up her accounts right there in the hall. Aunt Mary frowned at her. "Perhaps

77

I'd better see that you eat, my dear," she said, propelling Callie in front of her into the breakfast parlor. "You're as white as a sheet. In my day, we treated this sort of thing with castor oil." Callie made a strangled sound as she fought down nausea and managed a weak smile. Aunt Mary looked at her sharply. "Castor oil. That may be just what you need, dear."

In the breakfast parlor, Callie eased herself into a chair beside James. He had finished a hearty breakfast and was lingering over a last cup of tea, talking to Percy and Dee.

"It's true!" Dee blurted, staring at Callie.

"What is?" Aunt Mary asked, filling a plate to heaping and placing it in front of Callie.

"Dee and I were just discussing business," James interpolated smoothly. "We—with your permission, of course—plan to go to Scotland shortly so Dee can see the woolen mills for himself and make some arrangements with Angus MacKenzie."

Aunt Mary nodded approvingly. "Wonderful. I knew DeQuincey would take an interest in business as soon as he was old enough. My dear brother would be delighted at this turn. Of course you have my permission." She smiled delightedly at a rather astonished Dee, then turned and patted Callie on the shoulder. "Eat up and you'll feel better, dear. If breakfast doesn't do the trick, then we'll try something else." She whisked out of the room with a last approving smile at James and Dee.

Callie opened her eyes and stared for a sickening second at the plate of kippers and grilled kidneys in front of her. *"Uuuuuhhh,"* she moaned, closing her eyes tightly to shut out the sight while she felt so queasy. James whisked the plate away and put it aside. "Here, my girl," he said, putting his hand under her chin and tilting up her head, "what you need is some strong coffee." Callie shuddered as he lifted the cup for her and she sipped. She drank half the cup before he put it down. "Is that better?"

"I want to die," Callie moaned. "I'm *going* to die."

"No, you're not," James said briskly. "What you are going to do is drink this entire pot of coffee." He refilled the cup. "Here, drink up. Since Percy had mentioned you were to meet Captain Sinclair early this afternoon, I also took the liberty of writing him and postponing your appointment until tomorrow. I, uh, didn't think you'd be all the thing this morning."

Callie moaned in answer and drank more coffee. As soon as the cup was empty, James refilled it. "Callie, why in the devil . . ." Dee began, but James stopped him. "Later," he said, to Dee. "For now, could you feed those kidneys to the dog or whatever you have around? I'm sure when your aunt returns, she'll expect Callie to have cleaned her plate."

"We don't have a dog," Dee said, moving the plate in front of his place and absently beginning to pick at the food. Then a smile lit up his face. "This is really a capital development. I've waited for years for Callie to make a slip, and she couldn't have done better than this."

"Shut up." Callie tried to stand. "I'm going upstairs to die."

There was a crash at the door, followed by angry voices. A second later, the door to the breakfast parlor was flung open. Framed in the doorway was a very angry Captain Sinclair, a crumpled note in his hand.

"What is this, Miss Stone? This morning I received a message from Viscount Atwater and I have come to ask — no, I demand — an explanation." He caught sight of James at the table and drew himself up stiffly. "I believe we met last evening, sir," he said coldly and formally. "My congratulations."

"Congratulations?" James was puzzled.

Captain Sinclair nodded his head a fraction. "Miss Bramley's father informed me that Miss Bramley was betrothed to another — a distinguished gentleman of title, was the exact term, I believe — and since you were with her last evening and had her father's obvious approval, I deduced you were that gentleman." He bowed slightly. "I'm sorry I was so slow to recognize it. My congratulations." His eyes went from James to Callie and back again. "I thought we had an agreement, Miss Stone, but now I believe I begin to see how things stand. You seem to have quite skillfully made a fool of me. I can excuse my gullibility only by saying I expected better from you." His mouth was an angry slash. "My compliments — to both of you — and good day." He tossed James's note down on the table and marched out, closing the door heavily behind him.

Callie sank back into her chair, put both hands over her face, and moaned. It seemed the only appropriate response.

Percy and Dee stared from James and Callie to the closed door, and then back to each other. "I was right — Lud, what a coil," Percy said, while Dee nodded agreement.

James had Dee take Callie upstairs and turn her over to Brewster to be put to bed. Dee, Percy, and James decided they had no idea what the real circumstances of the situation were, and they wouldn't be able to unravel the tangle without explanations from Callie and Captain Sinclair. James pointed out that Callie was unable to explain, and Captain Sinclair was in no mood for conversation, so they decided to put explanations off until the next day. Instead, the men determined to make a day of it out in the country. James took Dee up in his curricle while Percy rode beside them. They toured the countryside around Bath for the day, visiting Sham Castle and viewing the town from the top of the hill. They came back in ample time to dine and get ready to attend the Upper Rooms for the evening. By this time, James had accomplished his purpose for the day—he and Dee were on the best of terms.

When they entered, they heard a loud voice echoing from behind the library door. "That can't be Aunt Mary," Dee said as John closed the front door behind them. "Who in the world's here and making all that uproar?"

"Mrs. Elliott is out," John answered. "Miss Bramley just arrived and is in the library with Miss Stone." They all stared at each other as a long, keening wail emanated from the library. "Which of us is brave enough to interrupt?" James asked, looking from Percy to Dee.

"I need to wash up and change," Percy said hastily, heading up the steps without waiting for an answer. "Need a new neckcloth, you know."

"I'm dusty myself," Dee said, looking at James, "but I wouldn't miss this for the world." He tried unsuccessfully to keep a grin off his face, then gave up and laughed. "I'm no coward—just call me prudent. I'll follow you in if you'll go first."

"Smart lad," James said with a laugh, handing his gloves to John. "Let's see what's going on."

Their knock was ignored. They could hear Venetia wailing behind the door. James knocked again, and when there was no answer, he opened the door.

"How could you? How could you have done this to me? You've ruined my whole life!" Venetia was pacing the floor, flinging her arms around, her face contorted and swollen from crying.

"Venetia, please," Callie said numbly. She was sitting on the sofa, still very pale and obviously not yet in the pink.

"May we interrupt?" James asked, closing the door behind Dee. "Is there anything I can do?" To his surprise, Venetia flung herself on him. "Oh, Viscount Atwater," she wailed, "I'm so glad you're here!"

Without thinking, James put his arms around her. "My dear Miss Bramley, whatever is wrong?"

Callie stood shakily. "Jamie, don't . . ." she began.

"You feel terrible, too, don't you?" he asked, putting one arm around her shoulders and pulling her to him as well.

"No, it isn't that, it's just . . ." She was interrupted when the library door was flung open as John announced a guest. "Captain Andrew Sinclair." Callie jumped back, away from Jamie's encircling arm.

Captain Sinclair paused a moment to look at her, a long, cold look, before he stepped inside the library. Venetia lifted her head from James's shoulder to stare at him. "Andrew! What are you doing here?" she gasped, then realized James was still holding her.

The captain's eyes never left them. "I should thank you, Miss Stone. When you sent for me to come immediately, you wrote that if I'd come at once, you could convince me that I'd understand the situation. You were correct—I believe I understand now." He gave Callie a withering glance. "If you sent for me to impress upon me that my assumptions of this morning were correct, then you've succeeded admirably, Miss Stone. For that I thank you. I had been willing to admit that I might have concluded wrongly, but I cannot deny this evidence."

Callie held out a hand to him. "Captain Sinclair, you don't understand at all . . ."

"I understand perfectly," he snapped.

"Captain Sinclair," James began, dropping his arms to his sides, "I assure you . . ."

"Don't bother," the captain said shortly. "Once again, Atwater, my congratulations, and good-bye to you, Miss Stone."

"You misunderstand," James said, walking over to a very pale Callie and touching her shoulder. "I admit I don't know all the particulars of this contretemps, but I'm sure there's a reasonable explanation." Grateful for his support, Callie put her hand on his arm and he absently patted it.

Captain Sinclair stared at the two of them in disgust. "Good Lord, man, have you no loyalty? You have the sweetest, finest heart in the land in your hand, and then you act in this way? I . . . I . . ." He stopped and controlled his anger, then spoke in a rigid voice. "I apologize, Atwater. I had no right to speak in such a manner. Good-day." He quickly turned on his heel and left, John ogling him as he brushed by. John took a last look around the room—Callie and Dee standing, Venetia standing next to James, James still holding Callie's hand—and shut the door. They heard the dull thud as the front door slammed behind Andrew Sinclair.

"My life is ruined!" Venetia wailed, breaking into

fresh tears and putting her head on James's shoulder. He looked down appalled as she thoroughly wet the front of his new superfine. "My life is over!" she wailed through her sobs. "I may as well go into a convent."

James looked at Dee in disgust. "Do you have any idea what is going on here?"

"I was just going to ask you the same thing," Dee said, looking in fascination at Venetia as she cried all the louder. "Percy was right: Lord, what a coil."

"An understatement," James said as he eased Venetia into a chair. Her sobs had turned into hiccups, and she was wailing incoherently.

Callie fell back onto the sofa. "I'll never touch sherry again," she muttered. "Venetia, stop that howling!"

"Howling? Howling? How dare you tell me what to do? This is all your fault, anyway!"

Before Callie could answer, they heard the sound of the front door again. Dee peered out into the hall. "Good Gad, it's Aunt Mary. That's all we need."

"Go distract her and try to get her out of the way," James said to him. "I'll take Miss Bramley back to Gay Street. Callie can manage to get to her room by herself."

"Many thanks," Callie said with disgust. "Your sense of gallantry is one of the things I've always liked in you, Jamie."

"You know me — ever the complete gentleman. Besides, I meant it as a compliment. Get up from there and slip upstairs as soon as Dee gets your aunt out of the way. Please be quiet, Miss Bramley." He pulled Venetia unceremoniously to her feet. "Hurry, Dee."

Dee gave Callie a grin. "You know, dear sister, that you're never going to hear the end of this. I love it." With that, he dashed out the door.

Callie stared after him. "Shut up," she muttered to the closed door as she stood up uncertainly. "Jamie, I'm going to be sick."

"No, you're not," he said, propelling her toward the door and peering outside. "You don't have time to be sick. Dee's got Aunt Mary in the morning room. Get upstairs in a hurry." He shoved her through the door and in the general direction of the stairs.

She wanted to say something cutting to him, but the library door was already closed, and getting to her room seemed as much of an effort as she could manage. Once there, she fell across the bed and put a pillow over her head. It seemed an ideal thing to do.

Callie didn't see anyone until supper. She thought about having a tray sent up to her room, but decided that was craven, so she went down. At supper, Dee kept giving Callie knowing looks which she ignored. Percy seemed blissfully ignorant of the scene in the library, so Callie assumed James hadn't said anything. For that, she was thankful. James himself was at his most charming, keeping the entire group amused with witty stories of the *ton*. Aunt Mary seemed absolutely delighted with him.

After supper, Aunt Mary asked if they planned to go to the Rooms for the evening. Callie begged off. To her surprise, James mentioned that he had met a business acquaintance and had agreed to attend a private card party. He had made arrangements for Dee to go along. "It will be good for Dee to begin knowing people concerned with the woolen business. Besides, Mr. Rolfe knew both your father and mine, so he's particularly anxious to further Dee's acquaintance."

"Rolfe? William Rolfe?" Callie asked. "I remember

Papa talking about him. How do you know him, Jamie? Socially?"

James made a face. "No, just as a business acquaintance. I *am* part owner of the mills, you know."

"I didn't think you bothered with the mills except to talk to Mr. MacKenzie occasionally when you were in Scotland for shooting. I thought you left all your business to the trusts."

"That's what everyone thinks." He laughed at her amazed expression. "I'm just full of surprises."

"Well, this is all very fine," Percy said, "but I think I'll go on to the Upper Rooms to see the crowd. I just hope they'll have something better to drink than that weak tea."

"Are you sure you're not going?" Aunt Mary asked, giving Callie a sharp look. "You look recovered enough, and I thought you might be expecting that nice Captain Sinclair."

"I do feel fine," Callie said hastily, "but I'd rather stay in until I feel better."

Aunt Mary lifted her eyebrows. "You're much too quiet, my dear. In my day, young people were full of spirit. But then, we ate better back then." She looked at Callie thoughtfully. "Perhaps you need a tonic."

"I'll be just fine," Callie said, beating a retreat to her room. The last thing she heard as she left was James agreeing with Aunt Mary and extolling the virtues of sulfur and molasses.

When Callie awoke the next morning, she was almost her old self again. She got up early and went down to breakfast. To her complete amazement, she discovered that James and Dee had gotten up early and were already gone. The two of them had accompanied Mr.

Rolfe to see about some kind of business, Aunt Mary reported. "Do you know what that dear James told me?" she asked Callie as she leaned conspiratorially over her breakfast plate. "He thinks Dee has the same touch for business that Matthew had." She nodded approvingly. "I knew all Dee wanted was a firm guiding hand. Atwater is just the man to give DeQuincey some direction."

"Jamie? A guiding hand for Dee?" Callie was astounded. "Are we discussing the same man?"

"Don't be snide, dear. It isn't becoming. I think you may have misunderstood dear James."

Reluctant to be snide, Callie let the matter drop. Instead, she determined to spend the day sorting out the contretemps between Venetia and Captain Sinclair, since she did feel responsible. To that end, she sent notes to both of them requesting that they call during the afternoon. To her dismay, the footman delivering the note to Captain Sinclair returned, reporting that the captain was not there and had left Bath for a day or two. Venetia sent a note saying she knew what Callie wanted to discuss, and she would be there in midafternoon. At least, Callie thought, one side of the affair could be resolved.

Percy came down long after breakfast and announced he was going to see a friend he had met at the Upper Rooms. He looked sleepy, and when Callie remarked it, he told her he had come late. "Then that dratted James came in practically at daylight and woke me up to ask if I wanted to go gallivanting over the country to look at weavers or some such. I told him in no uncertain terms that a gentleman doesn't need to keep country hours, even in a place like Bath."

"I'm sure the inhabitants of Bath appreciate your sentiments," Callie said, laughing. "Did you enjoy your evening?"

Percy nodded. "I discovered Miss Bramley at the Rooms, looking quite fetching, I thought. Since there was no one else there of consequence, we had a lengthy conversation. I found her to be quite agreeable and sensible." He looked smug. "James told me not to interfere, but I think he'll be pleased with my night's work. Actually, I was amazed at the extent of her understanding."

Again Callie wondered if they were talking about the same person, but decided not to risk being snide. Instead, she wished Percy a good day and decided to spend her time putting some finishing touches on a landscape she had been painting. It might have been only her mood, but it seemed that no matter how she changed the landscape, it never quite satisfied her. The truth of the matter, she decided, was that her talent lay in portraits. Her landscapes always looked rather like gray afternoons in the swamp.

Venetia was announced in mid afternoon, just as Callie had settled down to doing some preliminary sketching for the portrait she had promised Venetia. She was looking over some old sketches of Venetia when John announced her. "Oh, Callie, you're beginning on my portrait. How wonderful!" she exclaimed, rushing into the room, looking all the thing in a lavender gown with cream trim.

Callie looked at her. "Venetia, I do believe you've recovered.

"Oh, quite, and you know the reason why, you sly girl. Callie, I couldn't believe it — it's the most wonderful thing." She smiled broadly. "Thank you for changing my life." She paused and picked up the preliminary sketches. "I do wish that now you could wait and paint me in my wedding dress. Would you do that?"

Callie smiled back at her. "Your wedding dress! Venetia, how wonderful! Have you and Andrew made up your differences with each other and with your Papa? And without my help?" She laughed, "I thought if anyone could bring your father around, you could. He's seldom been able to deny you." She placed a sketch on the easel. "How do you like this expression?"

"Oh, no, Callie, quit making fun. You know I'm not marrying Andrew," Venetia said, turning the sketch. "I don't think this one will do. I look as though I'm pouting."

Callie dropped all the papers. "It isn't Andrew? Venetia, what are you saying? What have you done?"

"I haven't done anything except accept an offer." Venetia smiled smugly, then looked at Callie in amazement. "You *don't* know, do you? I thought you did. Actually, I thought you were the one responsible for it." she hugged Callie. "It's Viscount Atwater, you goose."

"Jamie?" The name came out a strangled sound.

"Yes! Isn't it wonderful? Papa is beside himself. I had no idea that Viscount Atwater held me in such regard. He came all the way from London just to see me, and then, poor man, he was too shy to offer for me himself."

"Jamie? Shy?" Callie finally heard the last part. "He didn't offer for you himself . . . what do you mean?"

Venetia laughed. "I mean he had to send his friend Percy to offer for me. Last night at the Upper Rooms, Percy told me that Viscount Atwater was quite taken with me and had come all the way from London just to ask me to be his wife. He said, in fact, that Atwater was *madly in love* with me. Something to do with wedding

89

bells." She sat down on the sofa. "And to think, Callie, I had absolutely no inkling."

Callie sat beside her with a thud. "I don't believe you're alone on that head. Are you *sure* this was intended to be an offer for you from Atwater?"

"Positive." Venetia nodded. "At first, I was rather insulted that Atwater would send an emissary. I thought he should have come to see me himself, and at least been a little romantic — you know how you've always wanted to meet someone romantic. I said as much to Percy, and he said that Atwater just wasn't the romantic type." Venetia giggled and smiled at Callie. "I made Papa come over to speak to Percy, and Percy told him that Atwater wanted to offer for me. Papa was a little shocked at the breach in propriety at first, but we discussed it later, when we got home, and decided that propriety didn't mean all that much."

"Venetia, surely you're not going to accept!" Callie had trouble getting the words out.

"Of course I'm going to accept, you goose! How often will I have someone like Atwater offering for me? Papa and I decided that the Viscount and I would probably rub along quite well."

Callie could see the conversation in her mind's eye. Jamie's finances had probably been discussed from shillings to pounds and back again. Callie could even imagine the two of them listing his properties and worth. "Venetia, I don't really think that . . ."

Venetia laughed. "Now, Callie, I know what you're going to say, and don't bother. I've quite made up my mind to marry the Viscount, and I won't be talked out of it. Papa had hoped I'd marry a duke, but they're too scarce to consider. Atwater is quite well fixed, and I think he'll do nicely. As for Andrew, Papa has convinced me that the captain is much beneath my touch."

"But you are . . . were . . . so in love with him."

Venetia regarded her patiently. "Callie, you're still full of those silly romantic notions, aren't you? What does love have to do with anything?" She smiled archly. "Of course I'm still in love with Andrew. Calf love, Papa says, and I suppose I'll always think of him fondly. But, Callie, you've seen enough couples to know that love and marriage have absolutely nothing to do with each other. I'm quite sure I'll get over Andrew, and he'll find a nice, plump tradesman's daughter to marry."

"Venetia, please listen to me. I don't think offering for you is what . . ."

"Hush, Callie, quit trying to change my mind." She gathered up her shawl and stood up. "I've got to go now, but we can have a long talk later. Just think how it will be when I'm Lady Atwater. I'll be in London all the time, buying new gowns and going to balls."

Callie made one more try. "Venetia, I really don't think . . ."

Venetia put a finger on Callie's lips. "My mind's made up, Callie. Right now Papa is drafting an announcement for the *Times*." She looked back at Callie's sketch. "Could you wait on this? I'd rather be wearing my wedding dress when you paint me. Unless, of course, Atwater wishes an engagement portrait. I'll have to ask him." She held out the piece of paper and looked at it critically. "This pose will be just right with a wedding dress. Papa says I'm to go shopping for it immediately, and I don't have to worry about expenses. Papa thinks Atwater and I should be married as soon as is seemly. By the by, I want you to be in my wedding—I wouldn't want to be married without you nearby." She laughed and put down the sketch. "Smile, Callie, can't you wish me happy?"

"Of course," Callie said through lips she could scarcely move. "Venetia, are you sure that . . ."

"Of course I'm sure." She pulled Callie up by the hands, then kissed her on the cheek, and was at the door before Callie could say anything else. Going out, she turned for one last word.

"I just *love* weddings, don't you?"

Chapter Six

Callie sat in shock, moaning quietly to herself. This was how Percy found her when he walked into the library ten minutes later.

"Still feeling under the weather?" he asked cheerfully. "I thought you had recovered, but sometimes it can take a couple of days. What you need is a little . . ." He paused and looked at the brandy bottle, then back at Callie. "No, I don't suppose so," he muttered. "Perhaps a nap."

Callie burst into tears. "It's a catastrophe," she wailed. "What have you done? How could you? Just how could you do this, Percy?"

"Do what?" He looked puzzled, then pulled out his handkerchief and handed it to her. "You haven't been, uh . . . that is, you haven't been imbibing again, have you?" He looked uneasily at the bottle.

"Of course not." Callie wiped her eyes and crumpled the handkerchief into a ball. "Percy, Venetia's going to marry Jamie!" she blurted out.

He sat down and stared at her. "Is she, by Jove? I didn't know things had moved along that fast, but James was never one to waste time once he's made up his mind."

"You didn't make the offer for her?" Callie frowned.

Percy looked indignant. *"Me,* offer for her? Why would I do a fool thing like that? After all, James is the one who wants to marry her, not me. I, for one, don't intend to get myself leg-shackled for quite a while yet."

"No, I don't mean that *you* offered for her. I mean, did you offer for her for James? A proxy? Is that the right word?"

Percy looked at her carefully. "Are you sure you haven't been nipping at the brandy again?"

Callie gritted her teeth to keep from saying something she shouldn't. She took a deep breath and began again, taking his hand and forcing him to look at her. "Percy, this is serious. Venetia was here a while ago, and she told me that last night you had a long talk with her about Jamie."

"I did." Percy nodded. "I thought if he really wanted to marry the chit, I'd help him along, if I could. I dropped a few strong hints. I'd say her father seemed most interested."

"Percy, Venetia and her father thought James sent you to offer for her. She plans to accept."

Percy jumped up. "Why would *James* send me to offer for her? I told you I ain't interested in getting married." He stopped, puzzled. "Why should I get involved in this at all? That's perfectly ridiculous. Lord, I hardly know the girl."

"Sit down." Callie forced herself to stay calm while he sat. "Percy, Venetia thinks that Jamie sent you to ask her to marry Jamie." Callie bit off each word carefully and spoke slowly. "She thought Jamie was too shy to ask for

94

himself and sent you instead. She thinks she's going to be the next Lady Atwater. Her father is drafting the announcement for the papers."

Percy looked at her, horrified, made a small choking sound, and reached for the brandy bottle. He paused a moment, then reached for two glasses and poured some for each of them. He swallowed the first without tasting it, then poured himself another and drank it before he spoke. "Oh, my God!" he finally said.

"Exactly my sentiments," Callie answered as she sipped her brandy. She grimaced and put the remainder on the table in front of the sofa. Percy looked at it, picked it up, and drank it down.

"Percy, maybe you shouldn't drink any more until we sort this out," Callie told him.

He looked down at the empty glass he was holding. "P'raps you're right. Can't think too straight when I'm foxed." He put the empty glass on the table and leaned back. "Can it be sorted out? That is, can we keep James from finding out?"

"I don't know. That is, I really don't know everything that's going on here." Callie turned to face him. "Now, tell me exactly what you said to Venetia to make her think Jamie wanted to offer for her."

Percy blushed furiously. "Well, perhaps I said more than I should have, but I was only trying to help him along."

"And lose fifty pounds?"

Percy looked stricken. "Surely you don't think I'd try to influence the outcome of a bet! That wouldn't be the gentlemanly thing to do at all. I was only trying to help James."

"Do you want to tell me about it?" Callie prompted.

Percy sighed. "As I told you, James decided to get married, and to that end, he came to Bath to court Miss Bramley. Perhaps then he was thinking only about the will, and maybe that it was time for him to marry and produce an heir. I don't believe he was set on Miss Bramley in particular — anyone would have done just as well, even you, if you know what I mean."

"Thank you so much for that," Callie interrupted dryly.

"What I mean is, he just wanted a *woman*." Percy stopped and blushed. "Not exactly a woman," he stammered, "it's just that when a man decides to get married, he always seems to settle on the first available one around. I don't know that females understand that too well."

"I understand perfectly," Callie said. "Please go on."

"I don't believe in love at first sight myself, but . . ." He paused. "Well, it wouldn't have been at first sight anyway, because he'd seen Miss Bramley before, so maybe it was at second or third sight, wouldn't you say?"

Callie closed her eyes and got a grip on her temper. "Percy, please get to the point."

He glanced at her, surprised. "That's what I was doing. The point is this — evidently when James saw Miss Bramley coming down the stairs here, well, as I said, he had made his mind up and she was available. The whole point is that he fell violently in love with her."

"He fell in love with Venetia? Did he tell you that?" Callie spoke slowly, as though it were an effort to get the words out.

"More or less. Do you remember when we escorted you to Miss Bramley's house? Right after you went inside, James told me he had heard bells ring."

"Bells? Church bells? Harness bells?"

Percy gave her a disgusted look. "No, wedding bells, of course. He said he was in love and he had never expected it to happen to him just like that."

Callie leaned back and closed her eyes. "Jamie, in love with Venetia . . . it's hard to believe, Percy."

"Well, it's true, and I was just trying to help his cause along by hinting to Miss Bramley that he held her in high regard."

Callie grimaced. "I think you might have hinted a little too strongly. It's difficult to get a marriage offer out of a hint."

"Not for some women it ain't!" Percy caught himself up short. "Begging your pardon, of course, I know you'd never do such a thing." He jerked upright. "Oh, good God!"

"What now? Percy, I warn you—I can't take many more shocks."

Percy looked stricken. "I was telling you what James said about the bells . . . well, there was more. I told him I'd do all I could to help him, which is what I did, of course, but he told me not to interfere because he'd rather do his own courting." He leaned back against the chair and closed his eyes. "I'm sure he'll never speak to me again."

"Probably not," Callie agreed without sympathy. "What are we going to do?"

"We could go back to London. No . . . that wouldn't work for you."

"No. Any other suggestions?" There was a long silence. "If we can keep Jamie from finding out any of this, I may be able to talk to Venetia and explain things."

"Are you sure she'll listen? I thought she was, um,

somewhat *distressed* with you because you had, well, taken Captain Sinclair away from her."

Callie's eyes widened. "Percy! I can't believe you're saying such fustian. Wherever did you hear that?"

"Last night, from Miss Bramley. Anyhow, that's what I think she was talking about. She said something about how her closest friend was a snake in the grass."

Callie gasped. "And you believed her? I can't credit you with that, Percy. Me, take Andrew away from her? That's the silliest thing I've ever heard, and she knows better than that." She gave Percy a withering glance. "You should too." Callie paused and stared hard at the carpet as she thought, frowning. "I think I can talk to her and explain things, but I'll need to do it right away. Do you think you can keep Jamie occupied until I talk to Venetia?"

"Of course."

Callie looked dubious. "I'll try to talk to her tonight at the Upper Rooms, or tomorrow morning at the latest. You watch Jamie."

"It'll be like a hawk watching a sparrow. I won't be away from his side for a moment."

"Good." Callie rose and picked up the brandy glasses and decanter. She was standing there holding them as James and Dee walked through the door. James looked quizzically at the decanter and glasses.

"Celebrating again?" he asked negligently, walking over to stand beside her.

"Just picking up," Callie said, turning her head so he couldn't smell the brandy on her breath. "What have you two been doing?"

"Visiting a few acquaintances," Dee said, sitting down beside Percy and riffling through the mail John had placed in a tray. "James, here's a letter for you."

James took the note and put it in his pocket. "Don't stand on ceremony with us," Callie said. "After all, we're almost family. If you want to read your letter now, go ahead."

James smiled, broke the wafer, and skimmed the letter. "My mother and sister are in Bath," he announced to them. "They're staying with my Aunt Cavendish and read in the *Bath Chronicle* that I was here." He pocketed the letter and laughed. "Mother is not too happy to have to read of my comings and goings in the newspaper. She suggests I might want to visit her, but I rather think it's a command rather than a suggestion. I hope it won't inconvenience anyone if I don't attend the Rooms with you tonight."

"Not at all," Callie said, while at the same time Percy blurted out, "Don't even think of it."

Dee laughed. "Sounds as if they'd rather have you gone somewhere else than with them, James."

"I did detect a note of relief," James said, his smile not quite hiding a hint of puzzlement.

"Oh, no," Callie said quickly. "We'll miss your company, but I thought you might find the entertainment in Bath boring after all the excitement of London."

"Devilish dull at times," Percy added.

"Believe me, London can be duller than Bath," James answered. "However, I imagine Mother and Aunt Cavendish will provide enough fireworks to keep me occupied." He paused at the door. "Percy, you and Dee try to see that Callie gets home without mishap. Judging from the past, you have your work cut out for you."

"I assure you, I always behave with the *utmost* propriety," Callie retorted.

"I've noticed," James said, giving her a grin as he closed the door behind him.

"Why does he always leave with the last word?" Callie sniffed. "Just once, I'd like to give him the perfect set-down."

"No flies on James," Percy agreed, "but at least he's occupied and out of the way tonight."

"Out of the way?" Dee looked puzzled. "Did I detect a wave of relief when you discovered James was going to be spending the evening with his family?"

"We may as well tell him," Percy said, as Callie shook her head vigorously and said, "No, absolutely not."

"If you don't, I'll find out anyway. I always do." Dee sat down where he could face the two of them. "I'm waiting."

Percy and Callie started talking together. Callie stopped to let Percy explain, but Dee got so befuddled from Percy's account that he stopped him in mid sentence. Callie tried to clarify things.

"Venetia thinks Jamie has offered for her. Percy seems to have given her the idea that Jamie was too shy to offer for her himself, so Percy was doing it. Venetia has, of course, accepted."

"Quit bamming me, Callie, and tell me what's *really* going on. No one in his right mind would do something as stupid as that."

Percy blushed furiously and cleared his throat. "It's true, Dee. Venetia thinks Jamie has offered for her, and she's already drafting an announcement for the newspapers."

"Good God!" Dee's voice was as horrified as his expression.

"That's what I thought," Percy said.

100

Callie rubbed her temples. "We wanted to keep Jamie from finding out until I could talk to Venetia, but there seem to be two other considerations."

"And they are . . ." Dee prompted.

Rubbing her temples didn't seem to ease the throbbing there. Callie shut her eyes. "One, Jamie told Percy not to interfere, because he wanted to do his own courting, and two," she paused and her voice broke just a little, "Jamie told Percy he was in love with Venetia."

"Balderdash," Dee said flatly.

Percy looked insulted. "It's true—I heard it with my own ears, and James ain't one to prevaricate," Percy said, "although I own I was as surprised as you are."

Dee thought for a moment, then made a face. "So in other words, you're just going to tell Venetia that James is in love with her and will probably offer for her in his own time, whenever that may be. All Venetia has to do is hold up on the announcement. And you hope James doesn't find out about the whole mess."

Callie opened her eyes and looked at him. "Correct."

Dee whistled low under his breath. "Venetia, bless her heart, never kept anything to herself in her life. No wonder you were hitting the brandy bottle. I'd have done the same."

Callie gave him a disgusted look and got up. "We were not, as you so delicately put it, hitting the brandy. I'm going upstairs, and I expect you to go with me to the Rooms tonight. I've got to talk to Venetia, and I know she'll be there."

"Stay around and we'll plan strategy. It should be interesting," Dee said with a chuckle.

"Don't you two dare plan anything," she said, stopping at the door and pinning Dee with a glare. "All we need is someone else adding to this muddle." She put a hand to her head. "I need to rest awhile. My throat aches, and I have a terrible headache. I must be catching a cold." She slipped up the stairs to her room, hoping she wouldn't see Aunt Mary. She felt terrible, and for some reason, she also felt that the only cure would be to throw herself on her bed and indulge in a long bout of crying.

Callie didn't feel like dressing up for the Rooms, but Brewster insisted on her lavender. Callie looked at herself in the mirror after Brewster finished — the lavender hadn't helped. She still looked droopy and dazed. "Onward and upward," she muttered to herself as she picked up her shawl and went to join Percy and Dee for the trip to the Rooms. After all, she *had* to talk to Venetia.

For the first time in memory, Venetia was not in attendance. Callie sagged against the wall and prayed that dear Miss Bramley hadn't somehow been invited to dine with Jamie's Aunt Cavendish. She could just imagine the uproar Venetia's announcement would make there. Given Percy's revelation about Jamie being in love with Venetia, she couldn't imagine what Jamie's reaction would be. Perhaps he would be delighted once he realized his courtship of dear Miss Bramley was a fait accompli. Callie didn't want to think about it. She looked around for Percy or Dee, intending to plead a headache and ask to be escorted home. She finally spotted Dee, almost hidden against the wall behind a potted palm. Keeping him in sight, she walked over to him, dodging a rather hefty man in the middle of the room who was standing there, looking around as though he were searching for someone in particular.

"Dee," she said, "I was hoping . . ."

"*Ssshhh.*" He pulled her behind the palm with him. "What do you want?" he asked in a voice just above a whisper.

"I want to go home," she whispered back, then wondered why she was whispering. "I want to go home," she repeated in her usual voice. "I have a crashing headache."

"Wonderful, let's go."

Callie looked at him in amazement. "No arguments? You usually want to stay half the night in the card room while I'm pacing the floor trying to stay awake."

"Well, I, um, have a headache." He put his hand on her arm and began walking toward the doorway.

Callie stopped. "That's what I'm supposed to say. What's the *real* reason you want to leave?"

Dee shrugged. "No reason . . . just looking out for my sister."

Callie rolled her eyes toward the ceiling. "Fustian!" She was going to say more when they were interrupted by the heavy-set man. "There you are, DeQuincey," he said, just a shade too heartily. "I thought I got a glimpse of you, but I wasn't sure. Are you enjoying yourself? And this lovely lady must be . . . ?" He let his words trail off.

"This is my sister, Miss Callista Stone," Dee mumbled, looking at neither Callie nor the man. His discomfort was obvious, but the man ignored it.

"I'm Horace Bickell," he said to Callie, "and I must say, I'm delighted to make your acquaintance, Miss Stone. You remind me so much of my own dear daughter." He smiled broadly.

"Mr. Bickell," Callie acknowledged with a nod. Before she could exchange any more pleasantries, Dee pulled at

103

her arm. "I wish we had time to talk, Bickell, but I was just taking my sister home. She's become rather ill tonight—the heat and stagnant air in this crush is terrible."

Bickell smiled at them. "I understand perfectly. I hope we meet again, Miss Stone." With that, Dee propelled her toward the door, leaving Bickell standing, watching them with an amused look on his face.

"Dee, are you and Callie leaving?" Percy interrupted their progress toward the door. "I've been talking to your friend Bickell, and he's invited us to his house later for a quick round of cards. Are you game?"

Dee grimaced and looked pointedly at Callie. "Not now, Percy."

Callie stopped and smiled brightly at him. "Why not now, Dee? What are you hiding? As someone in my family said to me earlier, you might as well tell me, because I'll find out anyway."

"Not here, not now," he said, glancing around.

Percy looked at Dee, then back at the crowd in the room. "Dee, are you going to go with me to Bickell's, or are you going home?"

Dee stood taller and gave Callie a defensive look. "I'll go with you. But first I have to take Callie home because she's got a headache. I'll do that, then come back here to meet you." His expression dared Callie to say a single word, and she bit her lip to keep from doing it.

"Capital," Percy said, clapping Dee on the shoulder. "I'll be waiting." He glanced at Callie. "Sorry you're not all the thing. Perhaps a good night's sleep will be just what you need."

"I doubt I'll get any sleep since I'll be worrying about talking to Venetia tomorrow. *I* seem to be the only one concerned about it," she added pointedly.

Percy looked wounded. "Of course I'm concerned. Can't you see that I've been distracted all evening? I thought a game of cards would be just the thing to take my mind off matters. Now you go right home and don't worry about a thing." He gave Dee a glance. "I'll be waiting." With that, he blended back into the crowd.

"Of all the—" Callie sputtered, searching for the right word. "I simply can't believe him. *He's* the cause of this bramble, anyway."

"True," Dee agreed, "but fortunately for him, he doesn't have a clue about it. Let's go." He took her arm and escorted her out the door. Callie waited until they were well away from the Rooms before she went on the attack.

"All right, Dee. Back there wasn't the time or place, but now there's just the two of us. Mr. Bickell seemed to know you quite well. I want to know what's going on."

"Nothing."

There was a pause. "Don't tell me that! If I have to, I'll go to Bickell myself and ask. You know I will."

"Good God, Callie, can't a man do anything without his sister butting in and acting as if he's incapable of taking care of his own affairs? I can handle Bickell all by myself, thank you."

Suddenly it hit Callie. "He's the man you've been gambling with, isn't he? How much do you owe him?"

Dee groaned. "Yes, he's the man, but I've just had a run of bad luck, that's all. It happens to everybody. I'll bounce back, you just watch me."

"How much?"

There was a long silence that grew thick. Finally Dee spoke in a hoarse voice. "More than three hundred

105

pounds."

When Callie finally spoke, her voice sounded as if it came from far away. "That much? Dee, that's more than your entire year's allowance!"

"Do you think I don't know that?" he snapped. "I remind myself every day. Several times every day, as a matter of fact."

"What are you . . . we . . . going to do?"

"My luck will turn, I'm sure of it. It's just a question of when."

"We could talk to Jamie. Papa left both of us more than we'll ever need, and since Jamie's our guardian, I know he'd be glad to take care of it for you. It really isn't much at all, considering the fortune you'll be getting."

"No." Dee's voice was harsh. "I'll not be getting James to get me out of something. My luck will change. You'll see."

There was a short silence, then Callie tried again. "I think you should ask Jamie," she said once more. "After all, as your guardian, he's got your best interests at heart, and I know he'd do it and not say anything."

Dee turned and looked at her, his face pale in the darkness. "I know he does, Callie, and I also know if I asked him, he'd pay every penny of it and consider it a trifle. He probably spends that much on gloves and doesn't even think about it. Two weeks ago I might have let him pay it and not worried about it, but since he's been here, I've gotten to know him, and . . ." Dee groped for words.

Callie smiled at him. "You've discovered that what I've told you for years was right — Jamie is really quite a nice person, and now you don't want him to think you'd be so stupid as to get yourself in such a scrape."

Dee smiled back at her. "That's right. It's rather nice to have a sister who can put words in my mouth."

"Hush, you, that's what sisters are for." She laughed and touched his arm. "You *do* like Jamie, don't you?"

"Yes. I never thought I'd care one way or another for the opinion of the loftly Viscount Atwater, but now I'd like for him to think well of me."

Callie reached over and took his hand. "If he knows you as I do, he'll care for you in the same way. I can understand why you don't want to ask him." She paused a moment. "Dee, please reconsider going to Bickell's. If your luck doesn't change . . ." Her voice trailed off, almost as if she were afraid to say the words.

"It will, I'm sure of it." He clanged the knocker and helped her inside while John held the door. "Has the Viscount returned?" he asked John. He looked greatly relieved to discover James was still out. "Don't worry, Callie," he said, ruffling her hair. "I feel a new day coming on." He turned and was gone.

Callie stared at the door as John shut it behind Dee. "Don't worry," she muttered in disgust. "I seem to be the only one around here who worries about anything. A new day, indeed!"

She didn't make it up the stairs without meeting Aunt Mary. After explaining that she had come home with a crashing headache and general weariness, Callie realized she had made a terrible mistake. Aunt Mary put her right to bed and sent down for warm milk and a tisane guaranteed, as Aunt Mary put it, to make her go to sleep in two shakes of a sheep's tail. Callie thanked her aunt profusely and promised to drink the tisane and milk just as soon as she had rested a bit.

"Nonsense," Aunt Mary said, "drink it right

107

now. You need your rest. You *do* look a bit peaked. I don't know what's happened to your health lately."

"I'm fine," Callie murmured, smelling the tisane, then deciding that sipping it would only prolong the agony. She downed the contents of the cup in one long gulp. "That's awful," she sputtered. "What on earth was it?"

Aunt Mary looked pleased. "A mix of my own herbs. I'm not going to divulge the recipe, but I will tell you the main ingredient is boiled leaves of ground ivy."

"I *do* feel sick," Callie muttered.

"Here, have some warm milk. It'll be good for you." Aunt Mary blew out the candles and left, wishing Callie a good night.

Callie had planned to spend a sleepless night worrying, but whether it was the effects of the ground ivy or the warm milk, she went right to sleep and dozed soundly all through the night. She didn't hear Jamie come in around midnight or Percy and Dee come in around three in the morning.

Chapter Seven

Callie was at breakfast when Jamie came down. He was looking particularly handsome in dark blue superfine, with a waistcoat of lighter blue embroidered with dark blue. "You're looking quite fine this morning," Callie said. "Do sit down and have some breakfast."

"Thank you for the compliment and the invitation, but I'm to have breakfast with my mother at Aunt Cavendish's house." He glanced down at his waistcoat. "I thought I'd better dress for the occasion, although Packard didn't think me suitably attired for breakfast."

"He thought perhaps a dressing gown?" Callie asked dryly.

Jamie laughed. "I think he'd have preferred that I skip breakfast altogether. Getting up early isn't one of Packard's strong points."

"Will you be back later?" she probed.

He glanced at her in surprise. "I do believe you've seen right through my schemes. I was going to ask if I could bring Aunt Cavendish, my mother, and my sister to visit you and Aunt Mary this afternoon. Mother was quite careful to point out to me that you were all of ten years old the last time she saw you."

"Of course I want you to bring them," Callie said with a laugh. "I'm anxious to see how your mother manages to keep you checked so well."

He looked insulted, then grinned at her. "Actually, I usually dodge her questions fairly well, but I will have to admit that she hasn't, um, probed into very many of my comings and goings. As long as I make it a point to visit her regularly, she's quite happy."

Callie glanced at him and grinned. "She must be unduly susceptible to the famous Atwater charm."

"Spare me the sarcasm," Jamie said, rolling his eyes toward the ceiling. "Besides, I don't get off scot-free—what my mother lacks in inquisitiveness, Aunt Cavendish makes up for in spades. She wants to know my every move. Sometimes I think she must be keeping a log of my activities. She even inquires after my health."

Callie laughed. "She's probably just trying to keep up the latest *on-dit* about you from the scandalmongers. She must like you very much."

"That she does, but she rang quite a peal over me. It seems Aunt Cavendish is quite put out that I'm staying here instead of with her. I'm going to have to be something more than attentive to make it up to her, so I began by promising to spend the day with them. Aunt has even decided I need to accompany them to the Pump Room this morning." He grimaced.

"Be glad she didn't want you to escort her to the baths."

He shuddered visibly. "She did. She wanted me to be there at six in the morning to go with her. She even suggested the waters would greatly improve my health. I informed her I was in

110

the pink of prime condition."

"And she believed you?"

Jamie laughed and moved his chair so he could look at Callie. "Has anyone ever told you that you were a complete minx?"

"I've forgotten it, but I'm sure you've called me that and worse in times past. Would you like some coffee?"

"Do you know you remind me distinctly of Aunt Cavendish?" He accepted the cup of coffee from her and sipped it.

"Really? I hope that's a compliment."

He nodded and chuckled. "Aunt Cavendish is quite a character—the complete opposite of Mother. They're so unlike that I used to think one of them was adopted. She isn't, of course. Mother says that Aunt Cavendish is a throwback to a maiden aunt somewhere a couple of centuries back. She's really a dear, though."

Callie glanced at him in surprise. "It sounds as if you're quite involved with your family. I knew you were as a child, of course, but I thought . . ." She stopped.

"Ah, admit it—you believe the gossip about the infamous Viscount Atwater. "That rakehell, that libertine, that wastrel."

"Quit bragging on yourself," Callie said. "I merely didn't realize you were still so fond of family."

He glanced at her. "Of course I am—family, and those I consider my family."

"I've noticed over the years," Callie said with an impish grin. "Your attentions have been noted and greatly appreciated by all in this household."

He had the grace to blush. "I admit, I may have

been a little remiss in personal attention, but you've never wanted for anything, have you?"

Callie laughed. "No, never. I'm just funning you, Jamie. Actually, I'm enjoying having you around now, and I do appreciate your taking up with Dee. He needed a man to take an interest in him."

"I like him," Jamie said simply. "He has the makings of a fine young man." The clock chimed and he started, drained his cup, then put it down. "Much as I'd love to stay and talk to you, Aunt Cavendish will have my head on a block if I don't manage to get there in time to eat breakfast with her." He turned at the door and looked back at Callie. "Have you noticed that being an aunt to someone over fifteen seems to give some women a certain ruthlessness?"

"Definitely," Callie said, laughing.

Callie went upstairs to prepare to go out, since Venetia and her father usually went to the Pump Room right after he had attended the baths. Venetia didn't partake of the baths, but she did like to visit the Pump Room, where everyone in Bath was on parade, seeing and being seen. When Callie came downstairs, John was placing several letters on the tray in the hall. "Two letters for you, Miss Stone," he said, handing them to her.

The first was from Andrew Sinclair, telling her he had returned to Bath and been informed that Callie wished to see him. He asked if he might talk to her during the morning. His letter noted that if he did not hear otherwise, he would call shortly before luncheon. Callie sighed and turned her attention to the second letter. It was from Venetia. Callie went to the library and sat down near the window, trying to decipher

MORE PASSION AND ADVENTURE AWAIT... YOUR TRIP TO A BIG ADVENTUROUS WORLD BEGINS WHEN YOU ACCEPT YOUR FIRST 4 NOVELS ABSOLUTELY *FREE* (AN $18.00 VALUE)

Accept your Free gift and start to experience more of the passion and adventure you like in a historical romance novel. Each Zebra novel is filled with proud men, spirited women and tempestuous love that you'll remember long after you turn the last page.

Zebra Historical Romances are the finest novels of their kind. They are written by authors who really know how to weave tales of romance and adventure in the historical settings you love. You'll feel like you've actually gone back in time with the thrilling stories that each Zebra novel offers.

GET YOUR FREE GIFT WITH THE START OF YOUR HOME SUBSCRIPTION

Our readers tell us that these books sell out very fast in book stores and often they miss the newest titles. So Zebra has made arrangements for you to receive the four newest novels published each month.

You'll be guaranteed that you'll never miss a title, and home delivery is so convenient. And to show you just how easy it is to get Zebra Historical Romances, we'll send you your first 4 books absolutely FREE! Our gift to you just for trying our home subscription service.

BIG SAVINGS AND FREE HOME DELIVERY

Each month, you'll receive the four newest titles as soon as they are published. You'll probably receive them even before the bookstores do. What's more, you may preview these exciting novels free for 10 days. If you like them as much as we think you will, just pay the low preferred subscriber's price of just $3.75 each. *You'll save $3.00 each month off the publisher's price.* AND, your savings are even greater because there are never any shipping, handling or other hidden charges—FREE Home Delivery. Of course you can return any shipment within 10 days for full credit, no questions asked. There is no minimum number of books you must buy.

4 FREE BOOKS

TO GET YOUR 4 FREE BOOKS WORTH $18.00 — MAIL IN THE FREE BOOK CERTIFICATE T O D A Y

Fill in the Free Book Certificate below, and we'll send your FREE BOOKS to you as soon as we receive it.

If the certificate is missing below, write to: Zebra Home Subscription Service, Inc., P.O. Box 5214, 120 Brighton Road, Clifton, New Jersey 07015-5214.

FREE BOOK CERTIFICATE

4 FREE BOOKS

ZEBRA HOME SUBSCRIPTION SERVICE, INC.

YES! Please start my subscription to Zebra Historical Romances and send me my first 4 books absolutely FREE. I understand that each month I may preview four new Zebra Historical Romances free for 10 days. If I'm not satisfied with them, I may return the four books within 10 days and owe nothing. Otherwise, I will pay the low preferred subscriber's price of just $3.75 each; a total of $15.00, *a savings off the publisher's price of $3.00.* I may return any shipment and I may cancel this subscription at any time. There is no obligation to buy any shipment and there are no shipping, handling or other hidden charges. Regardless of what I decide, the four free books are mine to keep.

NAME

ADDRESS   APT

CITY   STATE   ZIP

(   )
TELEPHONE

SIGNATURE   (if under 18, parent or guardian must sign)

Terms, offer and prices subject to change without notice. Subscription subject to acceptance by Zebra Books. Zebra Books reserves the right to reject any order or cancel any subscription.

Venetia's squiggles. Venetia wrote that her father had taken a sudden turn for the worse, and wouldn't be able to get out of the house for a few days. Venetia had several paragraphs about her total disgust at having to postpone her engagement party, but the doctor had given the family strict orders that Sir Dudley was not to be excited in any way. This was followed by a whole row of exclamation points. Callie laughed as she made her way through Venetia's atrocious handwriting. It seemed that Venetia felt her father had gotten ill on purpose, simply to keep his daughter from having a large engagement ball. "No one but Venetia," Callie muttered to herself as she tucked the letters into a drawer.

Dee wandered into the library then. "Talking to yourself again, Callie?" he asked, dropping into the nearest chair. "A sure sign of mental imbalance, you know."

"If I'm unbalanced, you caused it," Callie retorted. She peered at Dee. "Don't let Aunt Mary see you," she said, "or she'll dose you with whatever's on hand. You look wretched."

"I needed that vote of confidence," Dee said, closing his eyes. "Don't you ever have any *good* news?"

"Perhaps. Venetia's father is ill and can't be excited in any way. That means Venetia is stuck at home for days. This will give James time to visit her, and . . ." The words seemed hung in her throat.

"Do his own offering?" Dee asked.

Callie nodded. "I still can't believe that, Dee. Venetia and Jamie are so unsuited to each other. Still, if she's what he wants, who's to say what's right or wrong?"

"Are you sure he wants Venetia?"

"He told Percy he did."

Dee shrugged. "I'd have thought James too level-headed to fall in love at all, much less with a feather-brain like Venetia, but from what I've heard, stronger men than James have fallen under the charms of bird-wits."

"I'd hardly call Venetia a bird-wit, Dee," Callie said defensively. Then she paused. "Well, perhaps I could admit she's a bit scattered at times."

"Except where her interest is concerned," Dee said.

Callie looked at her brother with new respect. "I didn't realize you were so discerning. The thing that worries me so much is whether they'll be happy. I'm convinced Venetia doesn't care at all for Jamie. I doubt Venetia will ever truly fall in love with anyone."

"Except herself," Dee said with a laugh. "Callie, I know you too well, my sweet sister. You're asking yourself if you wouldn't be doing James a favor to meddle a little bit, perhaps let him know about Venetia, then he can move on to someone more suitable."

Callie blushed. "No . . . well, maybe. It's true, though, Dee. I'm just not sure that Jamie and Venetia will rub along together. It doesn't seem that Jamie is thinking straight."

Dee chuckled. "Better let things run their course . . . there's enough of a muddle already. Besides, what man looking for a wife ever thinks straight? Most men seem to reach a certain age, then suddenly decide it's time to marry and settle down. At that point, most of them simply pick the first available female."

Callie grinned at him. "You *do* realize you've just described Viscount Atwater, don't you?" There was a pause as they sat companionably together, then Callie brought up another subject that had been on her mind. "How was your evening at Bickell's?"

Dee ran his fingers through his hair. "Did you have to ask?"

Callie felt her heart drop. There was no point in berating him. "How much more did you lose?" she asked quietly.

"Another hundred pounds." He rumpled his hair again and gave her a crooked, embarrassed grin. "Percy went down for two hundred, but he had the ready blunt. I had to give Bickell my vowels."

Callie closed her eyes and took a deep breath. "What are we going to do?" She looked at Dee.

He shook his head. "I don't know. I'll think of something. Lord, Callie, I've always been lucky at cards, we all have. I always thought it was Papa's luck or something—you know how everything he touched turned to money. It's just a fact that you always win at cards, and I always have too, until now."

"It's true we've always won, but neither of us has ever played deep—or I haven't, anyway," Callie said. "It's easy to win a few pence."

"Pence, pounds, what's the difference? It's how you play." Dee stood and paced around the library, pausing by the window. "I don't know what's happened to me. I just can't seem to do anything right anymore."

"Hush that, or I'm going to start giving you some of Aunt Mary's remedies," Callie threatened. "We'll get out of this, just give me some time to think."

"That could be dangerous," Dee said, laughing at her.

Percy came in, carrying a letter. "Your man John

seems to have as many letters this morning as the mail coach." He broke the seal and skimmed the contents. "A note from our friend Bickell," he said, tossing the note on the table between the chairs. "It seems he wants us to know that we can avail ourselves of his hospitality at any time." He exchanged a look with Dee.

"Callie knows," Dee said, "I told her."

Percy sat down and stretched his legs. "That's a relief. I'd appreciate it if you don't let on to James, however. One of his favorite things to do is twit me about my losses. He, for reasons that escape me, seldom manages to lose."

"At least I have some good news," Callie said, with a glance at Percy. "I got a note from Venetia telling me her father is ill and none of them will be getting out for a few days. Perhaps I can visit her, let her know Jamie wishes to offer for her himself, and he can go ahead and do it." She stared hard at the carpet.

"Dame Fortune smiles," Percy said with a touch of relief. "Not that I dread James's ire, but, well, he *can* be rather mule-headed if someone upsets his plans." He paused. "Not that I wish you to tell him I said that, of course," he added hastily.

Callie laughed at him. "Not today, but I'll keep it in mind for future reference." She paused. "Jamie's coming this afternoon and bringing his Aunt Cavendish, his mother, and his sister. Are you two going to be here?"

Percy stared at her. "Have you ever met his Aunt Cavendish?"

"Not that I recall. Why?"

"If you had, nobody would be here," Percy said fervently. "I plan to be on the other side of Bath, if possible." He looked at Dee. "If you know what's good for you, you'll be with me. That woman will have you drinking the waters, and then she'll be telling you that you need to be in bed by nine o'clock every night. I'm telling you, she's a horror."

"Say no more," Dee said with a laugh. "We might as well go now. Callie, we leave you to cope." With that, the two of them left, planning a long day away from home.

Callie went to tell Aunt Mary about the expected afternoon visit, then busied herself with some preliminary sketches for a landscape. It was late morning when John announced a visitor.

"Captain Sinclair," she said, leaving her paints and moving to the sofa at the end of the room. "I'm delighted to see you."

He sketched a small bow. "Miss Stone."

As soon as Callie had seated him on the sofa and rung for some tea, Captain Sinclair pulled a piece of foolscap from his waistcoat. "I wanted to come by and apologize for my behavior, Miss Stone. It was unpardonable, I know, but I hope you realize I was completely distraught."

Callie smiled and handed him some tea. "Think nothing of it, Captain Sinclair. I can understand how you could misunderstand the situation." She paused a moment. "Have you heard from Venetia—Miss Bramley?"

Captain Sinclair opened the note he held. "Yes, and she tells me she has accepted Viscount Atwater, but she explains the circumstances. That's why I came to see you, Miss Stone."

117

"Oh?" Callie wasn't sure what else to say. "Exactly what has Ven — Miss Bramley written to you, Captain, or are you at liberty to tell me?"

"I'm sure it's no secret to you, Miss Stone. Miss Bramley tells me you have her complete confidence. She also tells me her father has coerced her into accepting Viscount Atwater, and," he paused and blushed a little, "she still loves me very much and hopes there will be some way we can continue our friendship." He put a wealth of meaning into the word "friendship."

Callie stared down into her teacup to keep from looking at him in astonishment. "Coerced?" she finally managed to say in what she hoped was an even tone. "Really, Captain . . ."

"Yes, I felt the same way when I realized how much my darling must be suffering," he said, "so I understand your anger, Miss Stone. There must be some way you and I can rescue her." He paused and glanced at Callie significantly. "If only her father could understand that my expectations have greatly increased lately."

"*Your* expectations have increased?" Callie realized she was sounding greatly like a parrot, but Andrew Sinclair quite obviously thought she knew something she didn't.

He nodded. "Yes, as I'm sure Miss Bramley told you, I was in a fair way to receive a rather good inheritance from a distant cousin, but I heard yesterday that his heir had met an untimely end, and the shock has put my poor cousin near death himself. I expect to hear at any time that I have become a baron."

118

"A baron?"

Captain Sinclair looked quite pleased with himself. "Yes, I will be Lord Easton, I'm quite sure of it. Won't my darling be pleased!" He smiled broadly. "Please forgive me for being so familiar about Miss Bramley, but since you know how the both of us feel, I know you'll understand."

"Of course," Callie said absently, realizing that she understood absolutely nothing of Venetia's motives. "Captain Sinclair," she tried again, hesitantly, "I really believe Miss Bramley is planning to marry Viscount Atwater."

He nodded and smiled. "I know it seems that way, Miss Stone, but it's all a sham. This is all her father's doing. I think she'll be able to cry off with the Viscount and accept me once she knows my expectations are to be realized. I'm also certain her father will cease to insist that she marry Atwater, a person she so obviously detests."

"Captain, I really think . . ." Callie began, but the captain held up a hand to stop her. "Miss Stone, my mind is made up. There's only one obstacle—I need to talk to Miss Bramley and tell her the news. That's where you can help me."

"Help you? How?"

The captain replaced the note in his waistcoat pocket and couldn't suppress a glance at Callie that showed he thought her rather dense. He explained patiently. "I need to speak to Miss Bramley and tell her all of this, Miss Stone. I tried to call on her, but I was refused—her father's orders, I'm sure. I did learn that her father is ill and will be staying home, but Miss Bramley and her mother will be going out this afternoon." He hesitated a moment. "Miss Stone, will you once again allow me to escort you out this afternoon so that I might talk with Miss Bramley?" His tone became pleading. "This is of the utmost importance to me, and I—that is, both Miss Bramley and I—will be forever in your debt."

Callie hesitated. "Really, Captain, I'm not at all sure about this. Why don't you just write her a letter?"

"She specifically asked me not to write to her. She tells me she'll get in touch with me after her engagement ball, but I don't feel I can wait until things have gone that far. I *must* put a stop to this engagement immediately. Miss Stone, I simply cannot allow Miss Bramley to be forced into marriage with a man who will not make her happy, a man who is a known libertine."

"Now see here, Captain Sinclair, Viscount Atwater is a most exemplary gentleman who has been much maligned." Callie's voice was icy. "I do not wish to hear any scandalous *on-dits* about him, and I can assure you they're all lies."

"Even the one about the opera dancer?"

Callie felt herself blush. "Really, Captain, I thought you had more address. Now if you don't mind, I have a painting to finish."

Andrew Sinclair reached for her hand and held it between his. "Please, Miss Stone, please forgive me. I'm so distressed that I hardly know what I'm saying. You know I'm not a begging man, but . . ." He stopped and started again. "Please, Miss Stone, this is very important to me. Please say 'yes.'"

He looked so troubled that Callie found herself smiling at him. At that moment, the door opened, and James walked in. He seemed somewhat surprised to find Callie smiling into the eyes of Andrew Sinclair while the captain was entreating her most earnestly and holding her hand in a proprietary way. "I'm sorry to interrupt," he said formally, "but Mother and Aunt Cavendish refused to simply stop by here for a visit. They wanted to know if three o'clock would be convenient for you and Aunt Mary."

Callie snatched her hand from Andrew's grasp. "Of course." She was groping for something else to say, but she didn't get the opportunity. James nodded briefly. "Fine, I'll relay the message," he said evenly. "Good to see you, Sinclair," he added with a brief nod. "Servant." He was gone, and the door shut softly behind him.

There was a short pause. "A strange cove," Captain Sinclair muttered. "I could almost like him if he wasn't making Miss Bramley so miserable."

"I think you may have things reversed," Callie said, still staring at the closed door.

"What do you mean?" Andrew's voice was sharp.

Callie shook her head. "Nothing, Captain Sinclair, but I think you're right—perhaps you should talk to Venetia."

He smiled broadly and grasped her hand again. "Then you'll assist me? Miss Stone, you've made me a very happy man. I know if I can just talk to Miss Bramley for a few minutes, I can convince her to cry off the engagement with Atwater right away. She loves me and I love her, so I'm sure we can persuade her father to agree to the match." He stood, still smiling. "I can't tell you how much this means to me, Miss Stone. After all, I'll soon be Lord Easton; I need to be thinking about settling down and producing an heir."

"Of course," Callie said, slightly dazed.

"Miss Stone, you're quite wonderful," Captain Sinclair said, giving her a very unexpected, quick kiss on the forehead. "Until this afternoon, then?"

"This afternoon?" Callie probed her memory, then started. "Captain, I cannot go with you this afternoon."

His expression closed. "I didn't think you would renege on your promise, Miss Stone."

"I wouldn't do that at all, Captain," she explained carefully. "You heard Atwater ask if he could bring his family over. I've already promised to be at home this afternoon for them, and, since there's a connection, I'm afraid it's something I cannot break. I'll be glad to accompany you any other time."

He frowned. "I understand, Miss Stone. This is merely a temporary setback. I'll find out when Miss Bramley will be out next—my, ah, informant mentioned that she and her mother may attend the Assembly, or perhaps take the waters tomorrow."

Callie smiled at him. "Either will be fine, Captain. Please let me know. I think both of us need to have a word with Miss Bramley."

After Captain Sinclair left, Callie tried to work on her painting, but she wasn't able to do more than stare at it for long periods of time. She finally gave up on it, went upstairs and told Brewster of the afternoon's expected guests, and sat unheeding while Brewster searched through her entire wardrobe. Brewster was finally satisfied with a pink muslin sprigged with roses and trimmed with pink ribbons. Callie put it on, sat unthinking while Brewster brushed her hair, and was

122

somewhat surprised to discover that Brewster had made her quite presentable looking. At least that was one good thing, she decided as she went down to the library, because she hadn't been able to think of a single way of solving Dee's problem, and she was really worried about Venetia and Jamie. She had decided Jamie should have better, but if he really wanted Venetia, he should have her, but then there was the small complication of Andrew Sinclair.

Once in the library, she got a sheet of paper to make a list of possible solutions. There were none. She got as far as writing Captain Sinclair's name across the top, crossing it out, and writing it again. She was staring at the paper in disgust when Percy and Dee came in.

"I trust we missed the fireworks," Percy said, sitting down on a red brocade chair.

Callie glanced at the clock. "I'm afraid you've returned just in time. I assume you're talking about Jamie bringing his family for a visit."

Dee came in the library door. "Do you mean we went to all the bother to leave, and they ain't even been here?" Callie shook her head, and Dee threw a letter down on the table between the two chairs, on top of Callie's scrap of paper. "There's a letter for James, and if I ain't mistaken, that's Venetia's scrawl."

Callie glanced at it. "It is. Where and when did you come by this?"

"I found it just now—it was on the tray in the hall. I'm surprised John didn't give it to James this morning. When I saw it, I thought we might need to discuss it. There it is—what are we going to do about it?"

Callie frowned. "Well, we certainly can't open it."

"No, but we certainly can't risk giving it to James, either," Percy said. "No telling what the chit's written down in there. We'd be right in the suds."

Dee grimaced. "Knowing what a bubblehead Venetia is, she's probably sent him the full program for the wedding."

"I'm afraid you're right. We can't give this to him until he offers for Venetia himself," Callie said, leaning back in her chair and looking at the other two.

Dee answered her glance. "We can't give it to him then, either, because he'll know what Percy's done. What we've all done."

Callie glanced at the note on the table. It seemed to have taken on an entity of its own. "We can't destroy it, that wouldn't be right."

"We could lose it," Percy offered. "I'm quite good at losing things."

"No, it won't work," Callie decided. "Venetia might ask him about it someday — that is, if they *do* get married. This marriage is worrying me."

"Is that supposed to be news?" Dee asked flippantly.

Callie shook her head. "No, this is really serious. There's something I need to tell you, but it must be in strictest confidence."

"Of course," Dee said promptly while Percy looked wounded. "Do you think I would tell something I shouldn't?" he asked in an injured tone. He blushed as both Dee and Callie looked at him. "Well, I won't tell if I know I'm not supposed to," he added.

Callie paused. "I hardly know how to begin. Andrew Sinclair came by, and . . ." She was interrupted by John opening the door and announcing carefully and very formally, "Viscount Atwater, Lady Cavendish, Lady Atwater, and Miss Merrianne Williford."

"Oh, Lord," Percy muttered as they streamed into the room. He looked around, but there was no escape. There was only one thing to do and he did it: he stood, sketched a small bow, and smiled broadly. "Lady Cavendish, Lady Atwater, I can't tell you how much I've been looking forward to seeing you."

Chapter Eight

Aunt Mary came in behind the others, and Jamie introduced everyone to each other. Aunt Mary and Aunt Cavendish sized each other up like two pugilists right before a mill. Jamie's sister Merrianne sat beside Callie, and Callie tried in vain to remember much about her. Merrianne had stayed in London with her mother for the most part, so Callie had seen her only infrequently, and then when Merrianne was very small. Now she was an extraordinarily pretty girl with large, dark eyes and dark hair. Callie thought it likely she looked very much as Aunt Cavendish had as a girl. Lady Atwater and Aunt Cavendish had nothing in common except their dark hair. Jamie didn't resemble either of them, Callie decided, but then, she had always thought Jamie looked remarkably like his father.

"I thought James would be staying with us if he came to Bath," Aunt Cavendish was saying, "but he tells me you've made him more than welcome here."

Aunt Mary gave her a frozen smile. "I'm delighted he thinks that. Of course, with his connection to Callista and DeQuincey, we consider him a part of our family. When we knew he was here, there was no question of his staying elsewhere."

Checkmated momentarily, Aunt Cavendish turned

to Callie. "I understand you paint, Miss Stone." Before Callie could reply, she continued, "I do hope you aren't doing all those wispy landscapes that are so popular. Give me a good, solid portrait every time."

"Exactly what I've said," Aunt Mary said, thawing. "In my day, every artist aspired to good portraits. I see no use for landscapes myself. A frivolous waste of time and paint." They both nodded in agreement while Jamie caught Callie's eye and grinned.

Aunt Mary had sent for tea and poured each of them a cup. Merrianne set hers down on the table between the sofa and the chairs and turned to talk to Callie. "I'm so happy to see you again, Miss Stone. Jamie's told me that you're quite talented."

"Paints all the time," Percy observed, "though I really thought James disapproved." He looked at James. "Didn't you say Callie's painting was going to have to stop?"

James squirmed. "What ever gave you that idea, Percy?"

"The other day, when we were . . ." Percy realized everyone was looking at him. "Oh, dash it, my mind's wandering again." He turned hastily to Merrianne. "Any *on-dits* from London? I haven't heard a single thing interesting since I got here." He waved his hand around to encompass the room and the town, and in the process, knocked over Merrianne's teacup. "Sorry about that," he said, producing his handkerchief.

Merrianne snatched up the papers on the table to keep them from getting soaked. "James," she said, glancing at them, "you seem to have left your letters here. I'm afraid this one has tea all over it." She shook the piece of paper Callie had used.

127

Before Callie could say anything, James reached for the papers. He glanced at the paper on which she had written Andrew's name twice, then glanced at her. She felt herself go pink. James looked at the letter and frowned as he tried to decipher Venetia's scrawl. "If you've forgotten your mail, we don't mind if you open it and read it now," Merrianne said. "I'm always forgetting about letters," she confided to Callie. "I either forget to open them or forget to answer them. Mama quite despairs."

"Neither of my children would get high marks as letter writers," Lady Atwater said. "You might as well open it and read it, James. You'll forget it if you don't."

"I never forget letters," James said, starting to pocket the letter, then changing his mind and breaking the seal.

Percy and Callie exchanged alarmed looks. "I believe I'd like some more tea," Percy said hastily. "How about you, James?"

"No, thank you," James said politely, unfolding the letter. "Percy, whatever is the matter with you?" he asked as Percy dropped his teacup and it rolled across the carpet.

"Nothing, not a thing," Percy said, chasing the teacup across the floor and managing to bump heavily into James's knees as he did.

"Here, let me help you," Dee said, jumping up from his chair, picking up the cup, and dropping it again. He made a face as the cup landed right side up and sat there. James stooped and picked up the cup, handed it to Percy, and looked quizzically from Percy to Dee. Both of them suddenly found something interesting to look at in the carpet pattern.

James started to refold the letter, glanced down at it, and then looked at it in earnest. His face became rigid, and he turned pale as he deciphered Venetia's handwriting.

"My goodness, Jamie," Merrianne said, "I do hope you've not received bad news. You look downright strange."

"No," he said through stiff lips. "Nothing of the sort."

"You're a complete goose," Merrianne said, walking over to stand beside him. "Has cousin Harold stuck his spoon in the wall and finally made it possible for poor Amelia to marry that merchant?"

"Merrianne!" Lady Atwater and Aunt Cavendish spoke together with Lady Atwater finishing the sentence. "Such language!" Aunt Mary and Aunt Cavendish looked at each other and nodded in agreement about the downfall of the younger generation.

Merrianne, however, was quite unrepentant. "Well, Mama, you know it isn't unexpected. Cousin Harold's been dying for years, and Amelia's been counting the days, poor girl." She reached over and snatched the letter from James. He reached for it, but she held it out of reach. "I'm not even sure cousin Harold could give you such an expression, Jamie." She glanced at the letter, then she paled and gave it back to him. "Oh, I am sorry, I didn't know it was such a *private* letter." She stood there almost openmouthed, looking at him. "Jamie, I didn't . . . who . . ." She stopped, then wailed, "Jamie, you can't marry someone we don't even know!"

There was a strangled sound from Lady Atwater. "Married? James, you've gone and gotten married?"

"No, good God, Mother, give me more credit than that!"

"Then what? No, not now." She glanced around at the assembled company and put a hand to her head. "Please, James, would you mind very much taking us back home? I don't mean to be rude, but I seem to have been seized by a sudden headache.

"Haven't we all," James muttered, glancing again at Callie's piece of paper with Andrew's name written on it. He folded the paper and Venetia's letter together and put them in his waistcoat pocket, then he looked around at everyone. "I suppose all of you feel something of an explanation is in order, so I will tell you that Miss Venetia Bramley seems to have accepted my offer of marriage."

"Bramley?" Aunt Cavendish asked sharply. "Dudley Bramley's family? Lord, James, are you out of your mind?"

"Please, Louise, not here," Lady Atwater said firmly, rising from her chair. She turned to Aunt Mary with the best smile she could muster. "I'm sorry to leave in such haste, but I'm feeling quite unwell. Perhaps you could visit us soon."

There was nothing for it except to see them out the door. Merrianne seemed especially upset and held onto Callie's hand. "Please come see me," she whispered as they left. "I do need to talk to you." James also had a whispered word for her as he followed his family out the door. "When I get back, you'd better have some kind of explanation for this letter. I know you've had a hand in it somewhere."

"No, I promise, I had nothing to do with this." She would have said more, but the others were waiting for James, and he left her with only a glance.

As the door shut behind them, Callie leaned against it. There was a very large and very sudden lump in her throat. She looked around to see Aunt Mary, Dee, and Percy looking at her. She knew she should offer Aunt Mary some explanation, but if she had to speak, she knew she would scream instead. For one of the few times in her life, Callie burst into tears, put her hands over her face, ran up the stairs, and slammed the door to her room behind her.

After a while, Dee knocked softly on her door. She didn't answer, so he opened the door and came in, finding Callie on her bed with a pillow over her head. "Callie, whatever is the matter?" There was no answer except a muffled "Go away."

Dee paid her no mind and walked over beside the bed. "Are you worried about what James will say to you? If that's the case, you needn't be—Percy has decided to make a clean breast of the thing and tell James exactly what happened." He sat on the edge of the bed and patted her shoulder. "I know we fuss and fight, but you know I'd never let James or anyone else say anything to you that would cause you distress."

"It's not that," Callie sobbed, her voice muffled by the pillow.

"Then what? Callie, turn over and talk to me."

"If I do, will you go away?" she asked, turning over and sitting up on her bed, holding the pillow like a shield in front of her. "There's nothing wrong," she said.

Dee snorted.

"Well, there isn't," Callie said, glaring at him. "You're in debt over your ears, Jamie's angry with all

131

of us, he's in love with Venetia and it's going to be a terribly unsuitable match, and . . ." she paused and her voice wavered. "Venetia's going to be unfaithful to him."

"I grant all but the last," Dee said, trying not to laugh at her distress, "but that's preposterous. How can you say such a thing?"

"She said so," Callie blurted out.

"She *told* you she was going to, um, break her vows?"

Callie nodded miserably. "She didn't really tell *me*, but Andrew came to see me today, and she had written to him that they should still be *friends,* and hinted that they would be very *good* friends after she was married."

Dee's jaw dropped. "Andrew? Lord, who'd prefer that . . ." He stopped, remembering that Jamie and Percy had told him Callie had a *tendre* for Sinclair. He patted her awkwardly on the arm. "I'm sure Andrew would never stoop to such a thing, Callie. You don't need to worry about that."

"It's worse," Callie sobbed. "I know Venetia doesn't love Jamie at all. Now that she's accepted his offer — that is, Percy's offer — he'll never find out until it's too late. We need to do something."

Dee looked at her sympathetically and produced a handkerchief. "Mop up, sister mine. We're not going to do a thing. James wanted to handle his own courting, and if this marriage does come to pass, I'm sure he'll want to handle this in his own way as well."

"Yes, but Andrew . . ." Callie began, then stopped. "Maybe you're right, Dee. You know how Venetia is, and Andrew is too much of a gentleman to stoop to such a suggestion."

Dee stood and smiled down at her. "True. Quit being such a worrywart. By the way, I may as well warn you that Aunt Mary is convinced you're ailing, and she's out in the kitchen brewing up something guaranteed to make you violently ill, if you aren't already."

Callie groaned as Dee went out the door laughing, blowing her a kiss as he left.

Percy met him on the landing. "Is Callie all right?" he asked. "I would have gone in to see her myself, but I usually make it a policy to go the other way when confronted with weepy females. I've found it's the only way to handle the situation."

"She's fine." Dee looked thoughtful. "Do you know, Percy, that I thought you were telling Banbury tales when you were telling me that Callie had a *tendre* for Andrew Sinclair, but now I realize you were right. I thought she was upset about James, but it seems she thinks Venetia is still in love with Andrew, and that's gotten her all upset."

Percy shook his head. "Can't figure females—never could. James doesn't think Callie and Sinclair will suit, but he says as her guardian, he won't stand in the way." He frowned. "Why do people who don't suit each other always want to get married?"

Dee laughed. "One of life's great mysteries. It seems as if everyone's going to be in tonight. What say you that we go back to Bickell's? For some reason, I'm feeling lucky."

"I'm for going anywhere, as long as we go before James gets back," Percy said. "We'll pick up supper at the White Hart."

Dee glanced down the stairs. "Too late to run, Percy. Here's James now." They turned together to face the man walking quietly up the stairs to where

133

they were. His face was grim.

"All right, you two, I believe you have some things to tell me." He glanced around. "I believe Callie also owes me an explanation. Where is she?"

Dee sighed. "She's in her room, crying her eyes out over Andrew Sinclair."

James bit his lower lip and frowned, not looking at the other two. "Are you sure?"

"Just left her. Although what she sees in Andrew Sinclair is a mystery to me. I never did understand what Venetia found to adore there either." Dee caught himself up short. "Sorry, James, I didn't mean that at all. That is, I'm sure it was just calf love or some such, you know how women are." Dee finally gave up and stopped speaking.

James shook his head. "No, every time I think I know how women are, one of them manages to surprise me." He put his hand across his eyes and rubbed his temples with his long, slender fingers. "Could one of you possibly enlighten me about the letter I got from Miss Bramley this afternoon, or is that too much to ask?"

Percy looked around. "Well, I was just trying to help you out, and you did say that you heard wedding bells and had fallen in love. If you recall, you also said you needed a wife. So there."

James took a deep breath. "I need something to drink. Then perhaps all of this will make some sense."

"We're going to the White Hart for supper, and then on to Bickell's for cards," Dee said, trying not to laugh at Percy's explanation. "Why don't you come with us? Maybe after you've had something to eat and drink, Percy's tale might be decipherable."

"I doubt that," James said dryly, "but I'm willing to try it."

Percy looked offended. "It makes perfect sense, but you're just trying to be difficult. In a few weeks you'll be thanking me for helping you out."

James and Dee looked at each other. "You don't need to say a word," Dee said, "I know just what you're thinking. Come on and have supper with us, then maybe you can go to Bickell's and show them a touch of the famous Atwater luck."

James raised a quizzical eyebrow. "I thought gambling was illegal in Bath. Does Bickell run much of a house?"

"No, not a house at all," Dee said hastily. "He merely has a few friends over for cards and a little casual gambling. It's not a hell by any means. I just thought you might enjoy the diversion."

"I might, but I doubt I'll go with you there. For some reason, I feel the need to get thoroughly foxed. I'll probably spend the night at the White Hart." James rubbed his temples again and looked down the hall toward Callie's room. He started to speak, then shook his head. "Let's get out of here," he said to the other two.

In her room, Callie lay on the bed for a long while, trying to think. She finally drifted off to sleep, roused briefly when Aunt Mary looked in on her, and then slept some more. She woke about ten that night, chilled, cramped, and starving. She stood and rubbed the worst of the wrinkles from her clothes, brushed her hair back from her face, and went downstairs to try to find something to eat. Aunt Mary was just coming upstairs to go to bed, and Callie met her on the stairs.

Aunt Mary looked at her sharply. "Callista, I do believe you should go take the waters first thing in the morning." She frowned. "Perhaps you might even want me to arrange for one of those electricity treatments."

"I'm fine, Aunt Mary, really I am," Callie said hastily. "I was just on my way to the kitchen. I'm starving."

"I'll help you fix something."

Nothing Callie could say would convince her aunt to go on to bed, and Callie finally gave up. Aunt Mary insisted Callie sit quietly while she prepared a late meal that would feed at least half a dozen. Then Aunt Mary sat right across the table until Callie had eaten at least three or four bites of everything there. "I'm glad to see you're getting your appetite back," she said with satisfaction, putting the remains of the food in the cupboard and covering it with a clean towel. "Perhaps you're on the mend."

"I am," Callie said, feeling thoroughly ill from eating so much. "I think I'll take a glass of warm milk to the library and read for a while before I go to bed."

"Fine, I had John lay a small fire so I could work on my embroidery, so it's nice and warm in there. Have him put some more coal on if you stay up long." Aunt Mary patted her on the head, handed her the glass of warm milk, and left, reminding Callie not to stay up too late.

Callie breathed a sigh of relief and poured the milk out as soon as Aunt Mary was safely gone. Because of her long nap, she was wide awake, so she did go to the library, intending to work on her sketches; but she found she wasn't in the mood and the light wasn't just right, so she kicked off her shoes, settled into a plump chair, and began reading the latest she had selected from the subscription library. She had smuggled it into the house as Aunt Mary didn't care to have what she termed "romantical novels" in the house, and the marbleized cover of the Minerva Press was a dead giveaway. She read for along while, absently hearing the clock chime, and covering her feet up with a throw as the fire dissolved into embers. She was completely unaware of the time.

There was a noise and the door opened softly. Callie looked up to see Jamie looking at her. "I saw the light and thought someone had forgotten the candles," he said, crossing to the fire and holding out his hands to it. "It's started to mist outside, and it's a cold drizzle."

"Build the fire up, if you want," Callie said, pointing to several lumps of coal John had left in a scuttle near the hob. "It's almost chilly in here."

Jamie tossed some small lumps of coal on the embers and poked at them until they caught, then put a larger piece on top. He stood and turned to Callie. "What are you doing up so late? It's almost two o'clock."

Callie looked at him in surprise. "I had no idea. I was reading and lost track of the time."

Jamie glanced down at the book in her lap and grinned. "Another lurid offering from the Minerva Press, I see."

Callie inserted a bookmark and snapped the book shut. "There's absolutely nothing wrong with it," she said. "I happen to like books like this."

"A romantic at heart?" Jamie put his cloak across the sofa and walked to the sideboard, pouring himself a glass of brandy. "Do you want something?"

Callie gave him a defiant stare and was tempted just

to show him, but instead gave him an honest answer. "No. I had a late supper, and Aunt Mary fed me enough for a dozen. I really don't care for anything else."

He brought the brandy over with him and put it on the table beside the chair. He sat down and glanced into the glass. "I really don't want this either, but I keep thinking enough of it will have some effect."

"Jamie, are you foxed?" Callie looked at him sharply.

"No, but God knows I've tried to be. For some reason, the more I drink tonight, the clearer my head seems to get." He put the glass on the table. "I thought I might go to the White Hart and drink myself into oblivion, but that didn't work. I went to Bickell's with Percy and Dee instead."

"You *wanted* to get foxed? Whatever for?" Then his last sentence hit her. "You went to Bickell's? With Dee? Jamie, how could you encourage him to go to such a place?"

He chuckled. "I didn't encourage him, and, besides, it isn't such a place — not a gaming hall, anyway. It's just a house where Bickell ostensibly has a few friends over for cards. Actually, it's a sort of shabby-genteel gambling house presided over by Bickell and his daughter. If I'm not mistaken, Bickell is something of a card sharp, but the stakes aren't high, and the play's probably reasonably clean." He looked at her and smiled. "Bickell has a good thing going and he doesn't want to upset things by bringing his game to the attention of the authorities."

"But don't you think the man should be stopped?"

Jamie shrugged. "The man's a cheat, to be sure, but on a small scale. In places like Bath, where there's little to do, you're always going to have someone like Bickell. To answer your question, yes, he probably should be stopped, but in three months there would be someone else in to take his place. Someone discreet, mind you." He smiled at her.

"You will watch Dee, though, won't you?"

He nodded. "As you know, I've already talked to him about going to Scotland. I think he'll be fine once he gets into the business and has something to occupy him."

"Will you take care of it before your . . . your wedding? You'll be busy afterward." Callie made an effort to keep her voice level, but it was difficult.

"I'll take care of it," he said, swirling some brandy around in the bottom of the glass. "Callie, not tonight. Let's talk, but not about Miss Bramley, or Captain Sinclair, or Dee, or my tenants, or the mill houses, or any of the thousand things that I have to see to. Let's just talk the way we did when we were children."

"We can't go back, Jamie," Callie said with a sudden sadness.

He looked at her over the rim of the glass. "No, but just for tonight, perhaps we can."

There was a small silence, and Callie began remembering a scrape the two of them had been in, stealing cherries from the kitchen before cook could pack them into boxes of straw for storage. They laughed, remembering, and then Jamie brought up the time they played being Henry VIII and practically decapitated the dog. One story followed another until both of them were laughing, and the fire was once again burning to embers.

The clock chimed three, and Callie glanced up with

a start. "I didn't realize it was so late," she said, putting aside her throw and standing up. She couldn't find her shoes, and she covered one foot with the other as her feet began to get cold.

"Go stand in front of the fire to keep your feet warm, and I'll find your shoes for you," Jamie said, dropping to his knees to search. He pulled them out from under the chair and brought them to her. To her surprise, he knelt and put them on her feet, then stood up, very close to her now. The candles were guttering, and there was only their flickering light and that of the embers in the room. He stood looking at her for almost an eternity.

"Callie," he said thickly, tracing her jawline with a long, slender finger. "How and why do things happen?"

"I don't know," she answered, both sure and not sure of his meaning. She leaned a little toward him — he was going to kiss her, she knew it, and she wanted him to. Venetia would have a lifetime of having him, but for Callie, there would be only this moment, and she wanted to remember it forever. "Jamie," she whispered.

He bent to kiss her, just a touch on the lips. She was not experienced — she had been kissed before, quick, hurried kisses at dances, and once in the drawing room, but she had never been kissed in the way he intended to do it.

He put his fingers on her face, gently turning it, feeling the softness of her skin as he traced the plane of her face from her chin to her ear. "Like this," he whispered, touching her lips lightly, at first in the middle, then at each corner of her mouth.

She leaned into him, tasting the faint touch of the tobacco he occasionally smoked mixed with the sharper taste of the brandy on his lips. He held her closer now, and she could feel the slight roughness of his skin where he had been shaven. She at first tried to sort each feeling, each emotion, and store it up as a memory, but as he kissed her more deeply, she gave herself up to the sensations and enjoyed them. "Jamie," she heard herself saying as from far away, and she heard him say her name in answer as he covered her face with kisses and ran his tongue lightly across her lips. He held her more closely then, and kissed her deeply, almost roughly, but she didn't care — it was what she wanted him to do. She wanted to melt into him, become a part of him, to taste him forever.

He was the first to move away, and he looked down into her face without saying anything for a few moments. She gazed at him, hoping he would say something that would make sense of her world, something that would let her know he cared for her. If he asked, she would forget Aunt Mary, forget Dee, forget Venetia, forget propriety. She would run away with him and live happily ever after.

"I'm sorry," he said, letting her go and stepping back.

Callie tried to swallow the lump in her throat. She turned away from him and stared into the glowing embers. "I'm sorry, too," she whispered, meaning every word of it.

Jamie walked to the window and stared out into the blackness, his hands in his pockets. "Callie, I . . ." he began, then stopped. "I know both of us have other entanglements," he said evenly, still staring into his reflection on the black window, "and I shouldn't have done that. I'll never speak of it to anyone,

141

I promise you that, and I hope you can forgive me."

"There's nothing to forgive, Jamie," she said. "As far as I'm concerned, things are still the same." It took more effort than she thought she could muster simply to speak to him. "It's late, and I think I'll go to bed now."

He turned and nodded at her. She was standing by the fire, her eyes enormous, her face still flushed, and her lips still swollen from his kiss. He forced himself to stand still. "Good night."

She smiled at him, and he had no idea how much it cost her. "Good night, Jamie." She moved to the door and opened it. "Will you check on Dee when he gets in?"

"I'll take care of it," he said. "Sleep well."

She closed the door behind her and he stared at it for a moment, then walked over to the fire and tossed the last lump of coal on it, watching it blaze up around the edges. He sat down in the chair next to the brandy bottle and stared at the small flames. He leaned forward as if in pain, and put his hands over his face. "Oh, God, what now?" he moaned softly to himself. "What now?" He sat up and reached in his waistcoat pocket for the two scraps of paper—the letter from Venetia Bramley saying she would marry him, and the other scrap on which Callie had written Andrew's name. He put aside the letter and looked at Callie's handwriting for a long time. Then he put both pieces of paper back into his waistcoat pocket, and proceeded to sit in front of the fire and drink the rest of the bottle of brandy. It didn't help that much—he was only mildly drunk when Percy and Dee came in around four o'clock.

Chapter Nine

Everyone except Aunt Mary slept late the next morning and, as a consequence, she was completely beside herself, worrying about breakfast, complaining that the cook was going to leave if something wasn't eaten, and muttering under her breath about the sorry state of youth in this day and age. Callie got up before the others and got the full force of the diatribe, not really hearing as Aunt Mary ranted. Callie had slept badly, haunted by nightmares of Venetia and Jamie, their future and all their children.

Dee came downstairs while Callie was still sitting at the table, sipping some coffee. "You certainly look wretched," was his greeting. Callie looked over at him. "However I may look, you've got to look worse," she answered. "Are you sick?"

Before he could reply, Percy came in and sat down heavily in the chair beside Callie. "I think James is sleeping off a head this morning," he said. "At least, that's what Packard was saying to John. Said the Viscount wasn't to be disturbed by anything or anybody."

"It's just as well," Callie said dully.

"I don't know what's the matter with him," Percy said. "James hardly ever drinks to excess. Of course, with him, it's hard to tell, since he's always been able to hold his drink." He turned to look at Callie. "Did Dee tell you?"

"Tell me what?" She looked sharply at Dee, who turned a dull red and found something interesting in the bottom of his coffee cup. "Dee, what happened?" There was a small silence.

"Silly of me to mention it. It was nothing at all," Percy said cheerfully. "Well, I really need to get out."

"Sit down," Callie ordered, glaring at him until he sat. "Now, Dee, I want the truth. Did you lose more at Bickell's?"

He nodded miserably. "My luck was going so good for a while. I was going to get back everything I'd lost, and then on the last three or four hands, I lost it all and more."

"More?" Callie almost whispered the word.

"Yes." He looked at her defiantly. "I'll take care of it, though. You don't have to say a word, and I certainly don't want you to go running to James about it."

"I hadn't planned on running to Jamie," she told him, "but you know I want to help you if I can."

He sighed and ran his fingers through his hair. "You can't help, Callie, although I appreciate the offer. Lord, if I only had your touch with the cards, I'd be in clover. As it is . . ." he let the sentence trail off.

"Lud, Callie, don't tell me you're a gamester," Percy said, reaching for coffee. "I didn't know that."

"Hardly a gamester," Dee said, grinning at Callie, "it's just that she always wins every game of chance

144

she's in. That must be my problem, Callie—you got all the luck in the family."

An idea sprang full-blown into Callie's head. "That's it! I know how I could help you, Dee. I really could."

"How? Callie, your allowance isn't any more than mine, and you won't have your money until you get married. It's a nice thought, but don't worry. I'll think of something."

She shook her head. "No, not that. You could take me to Bickell's." She waited to see his reaction. It wasn't long in coming.

"No, by God! My sister isn't going to go there."

"Why not? I've heard that almost everyone in Bath passes through there at one time or the other. Even Jamie said it was nothing but a shabby-genteel gaming house. I heard that Lady Lydell was there a fortnight ago, and no one seemed to think it was strange. I don't think anyone would remark it."

"I would," Dee said grimly. "My sister isn't going into anyplace like that."

"I will if I want to," Callie said, staring at him. "May I remind you that I'm of an age where I can go where I wish?" She turned to Percy. "Will you take me, Percy? I would consider it a great favor."

"I . . . I . . ." Percy stammered and looked from one angry face to the other, all the while trying to find a way out.

"If you don't take me, I'll ask Andrew," Callie said. "Which do you prefer? I know he'll do it."

"Sinclair? That stiff-necked Methodist at Bickell's?" Dee laughed. "That one won't do, Callie. Andrew Sinclair wouldn't be seen there, and besides, he doesn't have the money to go gambling anywhere. He's in worse shape than I am."

"Not any more," Callie told him with satisfaction. "His expectations are about to increase. His cousin died unexpectedly, and Andrew is in line to become a baron. From all reports, he thinks it may be very soon."

Dee made a face. "Andrew Sinclair, Lord Nonesuch. Callie, it don't bear thinking on."

"Lord Easton," Callie corrected. "He told me about it yesterday, and I think he's planning to settle down and become quite the country gentleman."

"One looking for a country lady?" Dee asked, giving her a significant look, then glancing at Percy.

Callie didn't see his look, as she had put aside thoughts of Andrew and turned her attention again to Dee's problem. "Quite probably," she said absently, then changed the subject. "Dee, are you or Percy going to take me to Bickell's? I'll only wager a few pounds to see how it goes. I have that much to spare, and if I lose, I won't ask to go again."

Dee and Percy looked at each other. "We might as well give in gracefully," Dee said to him. "She's as bad as Aunt Mary once she makes up her mind." He looked back at Callie. "All right, but only for a short while, and only a few pounds."

"And, for God's sake, don't let James know we've taken you there," Percy added. "Not that I'm afraid of him or anything, but I'd just prefer that he didn't know. He can be dashed irritable when he takes a notion to be."

"I won't tell," Callie promised, "but do you think he might be there anyway?"

Dee shook his head. "No, he said last night — or

146

rather this morning when we came in—that his Aunt Cavendish had instructed him to invite Venetia to supper to meet the family, so he'll be there all evening. If I read his Aunt Cavendish correctly, she'll be all night quizzing Venetia."

"Quite right," Percy said. "He'll be tied up for hours. We'll get to Bickell's early and leave early." He stood up and glanced toward the door. "Remember, mum's the word." He gave Dee a look and a smile. "Shall we go down to the Pump Room and watch the parade this morning? I saw one particular lovely yesterday."

"That's something," Dee said. "Luttell told me he stood at the window last week and counted eighty-seven females passing by and didn't see a decent looker amongst 'em."

"Dee!" Callie was shocked. "How could you say such a thing?"

He laughed. "Have you looked at the female population around here? That's one reason Venetia stands out—the rest of them are either fifty and fat or else stringy and on canes." He glanced at the look on Callie's face. "Except you, of course: I consider you an Incomparable."

She threw a muffin at him as they left and shook her head as the door shut behind them. She poured herself another cup of coffee and sipped it. "Men," she said in disgust.

"Any particular man, or just men in general?" asked a voice from the doorway. Callie turned to see Jamie standing there, looking very pale.

The feelings from the kiss they had shared the night before came back full force. Callie felt confused, her emotions a jumble, and she wondered just what to say.

147

Jamie was standing in the doorway as though nothing had happened between them, so Callie took a deep breath and forced herself to try to appear as usual. "Good heavens! You look . . ." She stopped.

"I know. Aunt Mary already told me on the landing that this morning I had a marked resemblance to death warmed over. One of her more charming phrases, I think, but probably accurate, given the way my head—and the rest of me—feels this morning." He sat down beside her and she poured him a cup of coffee. He ignored the sugar and cream and sipped it plain. "That brandy seems to have a somewhat latent effect," he explained with a wan smile.

Callie didn't want to look at him, afraid he might see something in her expression or her eyes. She looked down at her plate, studying the pattern without really seeing it. He had told her he was sorry about last night, so it must not have meant anything to him. She was being silly, foolish, and a thousand other things. There was a pause, and she spoke just to fill up the silence. "I'm sorry you aren't well."

He shook his head slightly. "I've felt worse other mornings. I should know better by now. How are you feeling? No ill effects from reading half the night in the library, I trust?"

Callie didn't get to reply. Aunt Mary came in holding in front of her a book with marbleized covers. She held it gingerly, by her fingers, as though it would bite her. "I found this in a chair in the library," she said in a frozen voice. "Callista, you know that books like this will destroy your mind. This drivel will cause the extinction of our race, mark my word. All of these *things* should be burned."

148

"Aunt Mary," Callie began, but Jamie interrupted her. "Oh, I see you've found my book. I wondered where I had left it." He reached over and took it from Aunt Mary's hands. "I firmly agree with you that these books are dangerous. Someone had told me about them, and I thought I'd read one and see for myself."

"Disgraceful, aren't they?" Aunt Mary said. "I'm glad to know this wasn't yours, Callie, especially since I've told you I don't want these things in my house." She looked at James. "In my day, young girls learned embroidery and household management. If you've read any of the disgusting occurrences in that—that *novel*, you can see why the world is in decline."

"You're absolutely right," Jamie said gravely. "I'd heard several people say something similar, and although I should have simply believed them, I like to find things out for myself. I decided I should read one and see." He opened the book to where the bookmark lay. "I really didn't get a chance to read all of it, but since I now know what kind of book this is, my curiosity is appeased. I'm glad you told me you feel so strongly about these novels—I'll return it to the subscription library today."

"No need," Aunt Mary said generously. "Read it through and see what printers are foisting off on unsuspecting young women." She gave Jamie a significant glance. "Just don't allow Callie to read it." She turned toward the door. "I'm going out. I ran into a very dear, old friend yesterday who's come to Bath for a cure, and promised I'd meet him after he took the waters this morning."

"Him?" Callie asked as Aunt Mary went through

the door. "Aunt Mary, did you say *him?*" There was no reply. "Jamie, did she say she was meeting a man?"

"That's what I understood." He was trying not to laugh, and gave Callie a conspiratorial glance. "That's what happens when you have novels in the house, you know. It's part of the general decline in morals."

She couldn't suppress a laugh. "Aunt Mary wouldn't appreciate you commenting on her morals. I can assure you there's no decline in that quarter."

He laughed softly and handed her the novel. "Here, take this book, finish it as soon as you can, and return it. Since your morals seem to be the ones in question, try not to head down the path to perdition too far."

"Words from the wise," Callie murmured, taking the book from him. "There's nothing wrong with either my morals or these books, thank you. They're very romantic."

"Your morals are very romantic?" Jamie lifted one eyebrow as he looked at her. "I'd never have suspected it."

"My morals are fine, thank you. As for being romantic, I suppose I am." She blushed slightly and stared at a picture on the opposite wall. "Maybe most women yearn for romance."

Jamie seemed surprised. He finished his coffee and poured himself some more. "Really? And do you think that most men *aren't* romantic?"

Callie shook her head. "No, of course they're not. I don't mean to castigate your gender, but it seems to me that men don't think of very much except waistcoats, horses, estates, and heirs."

He looked injured. "You do us an injustice, madam. A man would tell you that most women think only of dresses, parties, shopping, and, occasionally, their children." He couldn't keep a bitter note from his voice, and there was a pause when neither of them said anything. Then Jamie looked at her, a slight frown on his face. "Just what is romance, anyway? I think men suffer from a surfeit of obligations, and women always expect them to bring flowers and be forever complimentary, no matter what the circumstances. Sometimes it's damned hard work to be a man."

"I know that. Sometimes it's d . . . very hard to be a female, too. We've always got to look pretty and be charming even when we don't feel like it. Then there's the matter of keeping up the household, making sure the servants are trained properly, seeing that the food is ordered for the cook, and attending to all those thousands of things nobody ever knows about except when they're not done—that's no easy job, I assure you." She toyed with a bit of muffin. "As to your question, I suppose romance could be many things."

There was a long pause while Jamie waited for her to say something else. When she didn't, he prompted her. "Such as?"

She smiled at him. "I'm thinking, I seem to have painted myself into a small square and need more canvas." She took a deep breath. "Romance is, I suppose, taking care of all those obligations we were talking about not out of a sense of duty, but because one wants to."

"Good heavens, Callie, how prosaic. I'm surprised at you. I'd have expected you to mention flowers, moonlit nights, and sweet phrases."

"Don't be sarcastic, Jamie, I was getting to them.

151

Well, it is all those things as well, but it's more. I should think you could have sweet phrases and flowers but still not have romance. I want someone to offer for me in a romantic way—with sweet phrases, music, candles, and all that, but romance can be little things, too—helping someone across a puddle, trying to say just the right thing at the right time, just being . . ." She stopped in confusion, her face pink. "Jamie, I can't define this."

"Maybe you're talking about love," he said lazily, leaning back in his chair.

"Perhaps I am," she admitted. "I don't think you can have one without the other." She turned to look at him. "That brings up a subject I wish to discuss with you—Venetia."

He put his cup down with a clatter and stood up. "I really don't wish to discuss it, Callie. You have your dashing captain, I am to have Miss Bramley, and all's well that ends well. There's nothing to discuss." He turned and went to the door. "Please tell Aunt Mary I'll be out most of the day. I have some business to attend to, and then I plan on dining with Aunt Cavendish tonight."

"All in all, a full calendar," Callie said with an artificial laugh, trying to lighten his mood.

"I need to stay busy," was his cryptic reply as he turned and left.

Callie sighed and shook her head in dismay. She simply didn't know how to read Jamie any more. When they were children, it had been simple, but now he was so complex, she never knew what to expect. Perhaps she hadn't known him as well as she'd thought. He should be happy—he had what he wanted. True, Merrianne and his aunt had seemed surprised that he had offered for Venetia, but they would come around after they met the delectable Miss Bramley this evening. Venetia could be utterly charming when she wanted to, and Callie was sure that supper tonight would be one of the times Venetia wanted to. With another sigh, she got up and wandered into the main hall. The house seemed strangely empty with Dee and Aunt Mary out, and Callie had no definite plans until the evening, when Percy and Dee were going to take her to Bickell's. She decided to spend the day painting, since her art had been somewhat neglected of late, since the day Jamie fell in the door.

Putting aside a half-finished landscape, she decided to review the sketches she had made of Venetia. They still didn't seem quite right, so she got out her pad and pencil to try again. Instead, she found herself sketching a portrait of Jamie, capturing him as he looked when he smiled. The sketch was so good that she began transferring it to a prepared canvas, working through the morning, not hearing when Aunt Mary returned, and not stopping for lunch. John brought her a tray, and she nibbled from it while she worked. She had most of the canvas blocked in nicely when Dee came in and looked over her shoulder.

"A wedding present for Venetia?" he asked.

In truth, Callie had no idea why she was doing the portrait, except that she wanted to. "No," she said shortly. She didn't want to share this with Venetia. She had captured the look in Jamie's eyes when he was lazily laughing, his eyes almost sparkling, and his smile just crooked enough not to be perfect. This picture was for herself, not for anyone else, and this was the way she wanted to remember Jamie. It captured the essence of the boy she had played with as well as the man he had become. She didn't even want to share it with Dee. She stopped and, picking up a cloth, covered the canvas and turned to look at Dee, who was regarding her quizzically. "Wedding present for James, then?" he asked.

"Perhaps," she said to forestall any more questions. "Dee, when are we leaving tonight? And what does one wear to a gaming house?"

"One doesn't wear anything."

"What! Dee, surely nothing like that could go on in Bath!"

"No, dash it all, Callie, that's not what I meant at all. What I *meant* to say is that you won't have to worry about what to wear because I don't want you to go." His frown was fierce.

She regarded him coolly. "Dee, my mind is quite made up. If you or Percy won't escort me, I'll ask Andrew to take me. Now tell me, what time do we leave, and what should I wear? We'll also have to concoct a story to tell Aunt Mary—perhaps we could tell her we're going to the Rooms."

"I hate to do that," Dee said, sitting down on a nearby stool.

"So do I. With Aunt Mary, I always expect a bolt of lightning to come from the heavens if I'm not completely truthful."

Dee looked at her and grinned. "You're always truthful, so you shouldn't have a problem. I'm the one dodging lightning bolts."

"From Aunt Mary and from me," Callie said fondly.

"Let's go to the Rooms for a short while, just so we'll be truthful, then on to Bickell's. I'll wear something suitable for both places."

Dee sighed. "There's no stopping you, is there?"

"No." Callie laughed, and touched him on the shoulder. "But remember—we're in this one together."

"Unfortunately," Dee said with a mock grimace. "I'll see you later, then." He made a face at her as he left the room.

Callie turned back to the canvas, took off the cloth, looked at it, and smiled. Yes, it was very much like Jamie. She lifted the canvas off the easel and propped it face against the wall, then replaced it with a landscape. She had just picked up a brush to paint over the landscape when John announced Captain Sinclair.

"Painting?" Andrew asked, glancing at her smock and the easel. "I'm delighted to have caught you at it, because that's one reason I stopped by, and I was wondering how to broach the subject."

"The subject of painting?" Callie wiped her hands, removed her smock, then indicated Andrew should sit on the sofa while she rang for some tea and cakes.

"Yes, painting. I told my mother I was acquainted with you and that you were an artist. Mother knew of you, of course, since she's a bosom bow of Lady Arnow."

Meg came in with the tea and cakes, and Callie poured. "I did a portrait of Lady Arnow last year, I believe."

Andrew nodded. "Mother suggested that since I'm surely to be Lord Easton, perhaps I should have you paint my portrait while I'm in Bath." He looked at her in some confusion. "Might you have time to do this,

155

or do you keep a list and work your way through it?"

Callie stifled a smile. "Hardly a list, Captain. However, for you, I would be delighted to shift my schedule to accommodate a portrait. When would you like to begin?"

"As soon as possible. Mother suggested I talk with you as to what type of portrait would be best. I thought perhaps I should be standing. Looks more dignified, I think."

Callie stifled a grin, then thought for a moment. "Captain, do you have time for a few quick sketches right now? If you do, we could try two or three very quick poses, then select one later."

"Splendid, Miss Stone, but before we begin, I need to tell you I haven't been able to discover when we might talk with Miss Bramley." He touched the back of her hand. "You don't know how relieved I am to know I have your assistance."

She made a noncommittal noise in answer, then got her sketch pad and pencil, and began with Andrew standing with one hand on the back of a chair, glad to be doing something other than discussing Venetia. Callie was quick and accomplished, and caught the essence of the man in just a few swift strokes. She wasn't really happy with this pose because Andrew seemed militarily rigid and stiff. She next asked him to sit in the chair and sketched him there, his hands on the chair arms. Again, he was stiff and self-conscious. Callie tried again, posing him leaning with one elbow propped on the mantel. This one was better, in her judgment, but it still didn't capture the personality of the man. Callie sat him on the sofa again, gave him some fresh tea, and began talking to him about his military experiences. Soon he was talking with animation, forgetting she sat there with her sketch pad and pencil. She worked steadily, and soon she had it, she thought. She put aside her pad and told him she wanted to fill in some detail work on the sketches before she showed them to him for his approval.

After he left, Callie added some strokes to the sketches, then tore them off the pad and placed them on the sofa, where she could prop them up and look at them in a row. The last one was, in her judgment, by far the best. In the others, he was stiff and unnatural, but in the last, his face almost shone with enthusiasm as he described his adventures. She stood back and looked at them again, then decided to leave them until the next day, when she could look at them with a fresh eye. She had started to gather them up when Dee stuck his head into the room and reminded her that they were to leave early, so she needed to get ready. With one last glance at Andrew's sketches, she decided to leave them there, propped up against the sofa. No one would be in to bother them.

Callie had been gone only a few minutes when the door opened and Jamie came in. "Callie," he called, looking around the empty room. His glance fell on the sketches on the sofa and he walked around to the front of the desk so he could look at the pictures. He stood for a long time, leaning back against the desk, staring at Callie's sketches of Andrew Sinclair. He ran his fingers through his hair, almost angrily. "Why, why?" he muttered to himself.

Jamie picked up one of the sketches, the last one Callie had drawn, and saw she had captured an expression on Andrew's face he had never seen there before. She must care for Andrew very much, he decided, if she could show such caring in his expression. With something like a grimace, he replaced the sketch on the sofa, then leaned back against the desk to look at them again just as Dee opened the door and stepped inside, looking around.

"Is Callie in here?" Dee asked.

Jamie shook his head. "No. I don't know where she is."

"We're going to the Rooms, and I told her to get ready early." Dee came over to stand beside James. "What's all this?"

"Some sketches Callie left here," Jamie said shortly. "I imagine we'd better not disturb them."

Dee peered over the side of the sofa and looked at the sketches. "Lord, it's old Andrew!" he exclaimed. "Who'd have thought Callie wanted to paint him? Look at this one—tell me truthfully, did you ever see such a stiff-rump?"

In spite of himself, Jamie laughed. "Actually, no, I haven't. You shouldn't speak of the man so disrespectfully," he added more out of duty than conviction.

"Well, he is—stiff-rumped, I mean. Callie was going to get him to take her tonight, but Percy and I decided to." He stopped short, realizing he was about to say more than he should.

"You may as well allow things to take their course," Jamie said. "There's not much you can do about it."

"When it comes to Callie, that's true." Dee made a face as they started up the stairs. "You know how women are."

"I'm learning I don't know very much about

158

women," Jamie said shortly, as he went off to his room, leaving Dee staring after him.

"What a bammer," Dee muttered in astonishment. "This whole household is going to Hades in a handbasket."

Chapter Ten

Callie dressed in her new dress of cream-and-black print trimmed with black ribbons and lace. Brewster insisted on a black plume in her hair, although Callie had thought ribbons alone would be enough. As she glanced in the pier glass in the hall before going down, she was pleased with her appearance, and, more important, she had a good feeling about the evening. She would be lucky tonight—she felt it in her bones. She couldn't resist smiling at herself in the mirror.

Jamie came out of his room as she was standing in front of the mirror, and he smiled at her in return, that faintly crooked smile she knew so well. She shifted her gaze so she wouldn't have to look at him—he was in evening attire and looked splendid.

"Off to the Rooms?" he asked casually as they went downstairs. "I'm surprised the good captain isn't escorting you tonight."

"He would have, but since Dee and Percy were going, I thought I'd just go along with them."

"Oh, then Captain Sinclair will be at the Rooms."

"Of course," she answered absently. Callie was glad

they were actually going to the Rooms so she would be able to tell Aunt Mary and Jamie who was there and what went on—at least, what went on for the few minutes they would be in attendance. She glanced over at Jamie. "You'll be coming home late, I imagine."

"Probably." There was an odd note in his voice. They reached the foot of the stairs, and suddenly Jamie turned and grasped her arm. "Callie," he began, "there's something I . . ."

Aunt Mary came in from the drawing room, dressed to the nines in deep purple and cream, with plumes in her hair. Jamie let go of Callie's arm and the two of them stood there, staring at Aunt Mary. She appeared not to notice. "I'm going out for supper with . . . with a friend," she announced, "and I may not be back until late. Please don't wait up." Dee came down the stairs, whistling tunelessly, and stopped midway, staring. "Don't gape, Dee, dear," Aunt Mary said. "It isn't at all becoming." With that, she pulled on her gloves and pelisse and walked past them regally, John bowing slightly as she went out the door in a swirl.

"Good God, did you see that?" Dee asked in a horrified tone.

"Of course we saw that. We were standing right here," Callie said. She glanced at Jamie. "Do you suppose this has anything to do with the mysterious man she mentioned this morning?"

Jamie started to laugh, a rich, full laugh. "I'm sure it does. Aunt Mary in love. What else is going to happen in Bath, I ask you? Who would have thought it?"

"In love? Did you say Aunt Mary's in love?" Dee

asked, aghast, coming on down the stairs to join them. "It ain't possible."

"I'm beginning to think anything's possible in this place," Jamie answered. "Maybe it's the waters here, or the electricity."

"Perhaps the magnetism," Callie said teasingly.

"Who has magnets?" Percy asked, coming down the steps, brushing at an invisible fleck on his dark waistcoat. He stopped and looked at them all standing there, looking up at him. "What is it? Is something wrong?" he asked in a worried voice. "My cravat undone? Too many fobs?"

"As usual, the picture of sartorial perfection," Jamie said.

"Now see here," Percy said in an injured tone, "there's no need for sarcasm. This is all the latest crack." He fingered one of several fobs. "I personally don't like all this jingling and jangling, but in fashion a cove has to stay au courant."

"Percy, you're a marvel. No sarcasm intended, I'm perfectly sincere." Jamie laughed and clapped Percy on the shoulder. He glanced at the hall clock. "I must be off to collect the delectable Miss Bramley for our command performance. I probably won't see you until tomorrow." He paused at the door and glanced at Callie, a strange, shuttered look. She was trying not to look at him, afraid he would see her emotions in her eyes. At this moment, she hated Venetia Bramley. She forced herself to smile. "I imagine we'll have a better evening than you will," she said, making herself chuckle.

"Probably so. Give my regards to the estimable captain." With that, he was out the door.

162

"Who's he talking about?" Percy asked, checking his cravat one last time just to make sure it was tied perfectly. "Sounds as if someone has a screw loose, what with all this talk about magnets and captains."

"He was asking if Andrew will be at the Rooms," Callie said, then paused as a thought struck her. "You don't think Jamie suspects we're not going there, do you?"

Percy was satisfied with his cravat. "Of course not, and besides, we *are* going to the Rooms. I doubt anyone will think to ask how long we stayed there. Shall we go?"

They went out, walking together. They had elected not to take a carriage, since the night was warm and the distance was short. At the Rooms, they mingled for about a half hour, then met at the door and slipped out. Callie felt rather as if she were going to a clandestine assignation, and mentioned this feeling to Dee.

"Don't be a goose," was his retort.

Callie had imagined Bickell's house as something of her idea of a gaming hall, no matter what Jamie had said. She imagined secret knocks on doors, burly footmen hanging around, the smell of cigar smoke as the men drank and gambled, and ladies present whose appearance flirted dangerously with the demimonde. Instead, Bickell's was just an ordinary-looking house, another in a long line of Georgian fronts along the street. The door was painted dark green, and the knocker was in the shape of a fox's head. Rather than utter a password, Dee merely dropped the knocker with a loud clang and the door was promptly opened.

Once inside, they were ushered into a well-lit interior, with people circulating around several tables set up for cards and other games of chance. These people were obviously well bred, and dressed for the most part in the latest crack of fashion. There was no cigar smoke, but there were tables of refreshments—dainty slices of cake, lobster patties, thin-sliced bits of smoked salmon, crackers, and punch. Callie was amazed—it looked just like any one of dozens of parties she had attended. The only difference was that there was no dance floor, just a few chairs and some sofas along the sides for spectators, and in the middle, tables set up for various games.

They had just entered the main room when a lovely blonde girl came up and put a hand possessively on Dee's arm.

"Evening, M'liss," he said, patting her hand absently.

"I missed you last evening," the girl said, pouting prettily. "You said you'd be here."

"I *was* here," he said. "I was in the back and didn't see you." He gave her a rakish grin. "Don't think I'd miss saying hello to you if I had known you were around, do you?"

"I should hope not, but you still have a black mark in my book, DeQuincey. I expect you to stay with me all evening in payment." She looked at Callie in expectation, and Dee made the introductions. "M'liss" turned out to be Miss Bickell, daughter of the host, and she was just back from Paris. She told Callie she had been in finishing school there. As M'liss and Dee drifted toward a gaming table, Percy muttered in Callie's ear, "Looks like an angel, don't she?"

"She's lovely," Callie answered, her gaze following Dee and M'liss. They were a noticeable couple. "She looks so sweet and defenseless, though. I can't imagine Mr. Bickell allowing an innocent young girl to come straight from finishing school into this atmosphere."

Percy snorted. "Finishing school? Don't believe a word of that," he said. "The chit's been finishing, all right—she's been in a gaming house in Paris owned by Bickell's brother, and she's been learning the trade. I know it's true because Alverson told me, and he's always on the up-and-up."

"Good heavens," Callie gasped. "She looks so young, so . . . so untouched." She looked again at M'liss as she linked her arm through Dee's. "Percy, what are we to do—that wolf in sheep's clothing has Dee in her clutches."

"Don't worry," Percy said, glancing around. "I warned him, and he ain't exactly a green 'un. He knows all about girls like M'liss." He caught himself. "Begging your pardon, of course."

"How does he know about that?" Callie asked, fixing him with a stare.

He grinned at her. "I think it's male instinct. Shall we begin over here?" He led the way to a table set up for vingt-et-un.

"You're changing the subject, Percy."

"So I am." He gave her another smile and stopped by the table. "Dee tells me you have a touch of the fabled Stone luck. I hope to be dazzled by your winnings."

"I hope so too," Callie said with a grin.

Callie played several games and won consistently. Toward the end, M'liss talked her into playing cards with her—just the two of them—while Dee and Percy looked on. Callie was surprised at M'liss as she played.

165

She kept looking at Dee and making remarks about how inept she was at cards. In truth, she did seem to be only little better than average, and Callie beat her handily. It was on to midnight by then, so Callie refused the offer of another hand, collected her winnings, and prepared to leave. M'liss escorted them to the door, talking to Dee all the while, begging him to stay.

"I can't." He looked uncomfortable and glanced at Callie. "I need to see my sister home."

"But she will be safe with Percy. Please stay awhile and talk to me." She batted her eyes and pouted prettily.

"I'm sorry," Callie interrupted, "but Dee really does need to see me home. It would be most improper for Percy to walk me home alone." To Callie's surprise, Dee looked relieved.

"But you will come back tomorrow?" Again the little pout.

"Either then or the next night," Callie said. "Shall we go, Dee? I'm quite tired."

Once outside, Callie couldn't resist. "I didn't know you had an admirer, Dee." She couldn't see his face in the moonlight, but she knew he was blushing, and he stammered slightly as he denied it.

"Don't care for the girl at all, Callie, I promise. I don't know why she dangles after me every time I go there. I've never said a thing that would cause her to have any ideas at all."

"Maybe she's trying to get you into deeper play," Percy said. "She's a sharp 'un, that one is. I'd watch out, both of you."

"Why should I be concerned?" Callie asked.

"I'm sure she could cause no problem for me."

Percy shook his head. "Remember what I told you. She ain't what she seems to be — or wants people to think she is. When you get down to brass tacks, she's trained to be a cardsharp."

Callie chuckled. "I had no idea you were such a worrywart, Percy. Still, there's no reason for me to watch out. I don't intend to get involved deeply." She turned to Dee. "Feel this purse, Dee. I think with two or three more trips, we'll have enough to pay off what you owe."

Dee hefted the purse. "If we use the whole thing as stakes, we can do it tomorrow night. I'd rather do that, before James finds out what you're doing."

"Let him find out," Callie said defiantly. "I'm old enough to do what I wish, and if I wish to go to Bickell's, Jamie can't do a thing about it."

"Lord, I hope you're right," Percy muttered. "When he gets up in the boughs, everyone in sight dives for cover."

"Well, *I* don't." Callie said. "Besides, I don't remember Jamie as being that way. He was always good-natured . . . so much so that his father always thought he didn't care about much of anything."

"His father was wrong on that count, along with some other ones," Percy answered. "I suppose James cares about things more than anyone I know. That's why he's always running around taking care of mill workers, tenants, his family, and Lord knows who else."

"He told me that was just responsible business," Dee said. "I mean, taking good care of the mill workers and tenants."

167

"All a hum, that talk about business," Percy said. "He does it because he cares about them, and he won't even let them tell anyone that he does it. Tries his best to make the trustees think he's nothing but a dandy and a fop. And they do." Percy paused. "His father hurt him badly by having such a low opinion of him."

"I remember his father always felt that way," Callie said. "No matter what Jamie did, it wasn't good enough. I think he finally just gave up trying to please his father when he was about ten. That summer, he decided to do whatever he wanted to." Callie paused and smiled, remembering. "We were in scrapes all summer."

They reached the door and clanged the knocker so John would open it. "Don't tell James I said anything about him and his father," Percy said. "He doesn't like people to know. He wouldn't care, of course, since you're family, but . . ."

"We understand," Dee said. "Lord, Percy, do you think we're a bunch of tattlers?" He shut the door behind him. "Are we still on to watch the races tomorrow?"

Percy nodded and they all went upstairs together. Callie stopped by Aunt Mary's door and knocked softly. She told herself she wanted to check on Aunt Mary, but, with a smile, admitted to herself that she really was consumed with curiosity. When she went in, Aunt Mary was propped up in bed, so Callie sat on the edge of the bed. There was something hard pressing against her leg, and she reached down to move it. To her surprise, there was a novel hidden beneath the counterpane. Callie instantly recognized the marbleized cover, and, as Aunt Mary snatched it away, recognized the title as one of the more lurid romances.

"Aunt Mary! I can't believe this of you!"

Aunt Mary was all blushes and confusion. "I merely wanted to see what all the fuss was about," she said. "After all, as James pointed out, one must have an *informed* opinion." She stuffed the book under her pillow. "Isn't it time for you to be in bed? Whatever do you mean, coming in at this time of the night? Callista, you must think of your reputation. In my day, girls weren't allowed to roam the country unsupervised as they are now." She shook her head until the ribbons on her cap danced. "I don't know what the world's coming to."

Callie laughed. "I was thoroughly supervised, as you well know. I was with Percy and Dee, and neither one of them let me out of their sight for an instant. My reputation is quite intact."

"I won't be for long if you gallivant all over the country at all hours." Aunt Mary yawned. "It's really time for me to go to sleep. Good night, dear."

"I just came by to ask about your evening. Did you have an enjoyable time with your *friend?* Where did you go?"

"I had a lovely time." Aunt Mary pounded her pillow to get it just right, and snuggled down in the bed. "Close the door as you leave. Good night, dear."

"I suppose I could call that a hint," Callie said, leaning down and kissing her aunt's cheek. "Don't think you can cozen me, Aunt. I mean to find out about your comings and goings. After all, we can't allow you to roam around the country unsupervised, can we?"

Aunt Mary laughed and kissed her back. "Go to

bed, you minx, and keep in mind that old ladies can do whatever they want. They've earned the right. Blow out my candle for me, will you?"

Callie closed the door behind her and started down the hall toward her room. She heard a noise behind Jamie's door and paused. He must be back from introducing Venetia to his family. There was a tightness in Callie's throat as she imagined the scene: Venetia dressed beautifully and looking like an angel, on her best behavior as she charmed everyone, including Jamie. Sudden tears filled her eyes, and she ran to her room and shut the door, leaning against it until the lump in her throat went away.

"Are you all right, Miss Stone?" It was Brewster, sitting in the corner, waiting to help Callie to bed.

Callie forced her voice to be level and took a deep breath. "I'm fine, Brewster. I'm sorry you had to wait up; I should have told you I'd be in late. Go on to bed and I'll see to myself."

Brewster was having none of that. To Callie's occasional irritation, Brewster was a firm believer in doing one's duty. "Since I'm here," she said, "I might as well help. Your new dress needs to be put in the clothespress." Callie grimaced. Her usual method of getting ready for bed was to undress and drape all her clothes over the back of the nearest chair, a practice guaranteed to send Brewster into fits.

"All right." It was easier to give in than it was to try to argue with Brewster. The dress was smoothed and put carefully in the clothespress, Callie's hair was brushed until it shone, and the bed was warmed before Brewster felt her duty had been done. "There," she finally said with satisfaction as Callie stepped up into her bed. On her part, Callie breathed a sigh of relief as Brewster left. She really needed to be firmer with Brewster, she thought to herself, but it was difficult to be overly firm with someone who had dressed you since you were in leading-strings. She blew out the candle and leaned back against the pillows, reviewing the evening.

She thought some about Bickell's and M'liss, but most of the time she kept manufacturing pictures in her mind: Jamie introducing Venetia to everyone, Venetia putting her hand familiarly on Jamie's arm, Venetia and Jamie getting married, Venetia looking beautiful in her wedding dress, Jamie being happy and proud, then Venetia meeting Andrew. She could see it all in her mind, every detail, every gesture, every emotion.

The candle wavered as it burned down, so Callie reached into the drawer of her bedside table, got another, and replaced the guttering stub with a fresh candle. It would last for several hours, she thought as she lay back down. At this rate, she could imagine Jamie and Venetia into their old age.

Callie bit her lower lip as she worried. Jamie wanted Venetia and fancied himself in love with her. Percy had told her that much. Venetia certainly didn't care for anything except money and a title. Jamie had to know that. Did he love Venetia so much that nothing else mattered? If he did love her that much, how would it affect him when Venetia resumed her friendship with Andrew?

She sat up abruptly in bed. Jamie didn't deserve this. She couldn't let this happen—Jamie had to be

171

warned that Venetia didn't love him and wouldn't make a suitable wife.

Before she could change her mind, Callie threw aside the covers and put on her dressing gown. She was across the hall and knocking softly on Jamie's door before she gave herself time to think what she was doing.

"Jamie," she whispered, knocking softly again.

The door opened and Packard stood there, looking stiff and disapproving. Obviously he felt propriety was breached when a girl in a dressing gown knocked on his master's bedroom door after midnight. "Yes?" he asked icily, looking down at her.

Callie looked over his shoulder and saw Jamie standing there, taking the studs from his cuffs. He had taken them from his shirt front and it was open, his cravat dangling around his neck. His hair was rumpled, and he looked very much as he had when he was ten and was Callie's best friend in the whole world. She forced herself to look back into Packard's disapproving eyes. "Yes?" he asked again, his voice no warmer than before.

"Nothing," Callie stammered. "I needed to speak to Dee, and thought I heard him in here. If you see him, please tell him."

"Certainly," Packard said, his tone indicating that he didn't think he would be seeing Dee wandering the halls after midnight.

Callie slipped across the hall, feeling somewhat like a convicted felon, and closed the door behind her. It had been a ridiculous idea, anyway—Jamie's life was his own, and he was certainly old enough to make his own mistakes. After all, he had been on the town long enough to know the likes of Venetia Bramley. Wearily, Callie took off her dressing gown and crawled back into bed. The candle was still burning.

She was considering a trip to the kitchen to get some disgusting warm milk when there was a soft knock on her door. "Callie," someone whispered, and opened the door. "I was afraid you were asleep," Jamie said in a whisper, walking in.

"I couldn't sleep." Callie sat up in bed as Jamie got the chair from her dressing table and placed it next to the bed. He sat down beside her and smiled at her. Callie couldn't look at him.

"What's the matter?" he asked softly. "Do you need me?"

She wanted to scream yes, she did need him, but there was no possibility of that. Instead, she forced herself to smile at him and answer. "I just couldn't sleep and heard a noise from your room. I thought perhaps you couldn't sleep either."

He chuckled and touched her hand where it lay on top of the counterpane. "So you thought we'd just stay up together all night? Not such a bad idea, that."

Callie moved her hand just away from his touch. "As a matter of intellectual curiosity," she said lightly, "how was your evening?"

"As I expected," he said, leaning back in the chair. "I knew Miss Bramley would be quite charming, and she was. Mother was charmed, Merrianne was enchanted, and even Aunt Cavendish decided to tolerate her. All in all, they quite approved of her." He paused. "How was your evening?"

Callie's head snapped up. "My evening?" Had Percy

173

or Dee let something slip to Jamie? "What about my evening?"

"Did you enjoy yourself? And the captain, was he his attentive and romantic self?"

"Oh, yes, definitely. I had a very good evening." This was dangerous ground, and it was time to change the subject. Callie wondered how she could talk to him about Venetia. From the way he spoke, Venetia had thoroughly charmed him as well. "Jamie," she said abruptly, "do you think you're ready to get married?"

He laughed. "Oh, so that's what you wanted—a guardian to ward tête-à-tête." His expression grew serious. "You do realize you're not asking an expert on the subject of love and marriage, don't you? But since it's you, I'll try to answer your question." He ran his fingers through his hair as he thought. "I don't really know, and that's not much of an answer, I realize. Does anyone ever *know* when to get married? I suppose one weighs all the factors for and against, and if the prospect is favorable, then . . ." His voice trailed off, and he looked at her intently. "Why do you ask— do you think you're ready to get married?"

"Me? I wasn't thinking about whether or not I was ready to get married. I was asking because I was concerned about a friend."

He raised an eyebrow and smiled. "Ah, a close friend, perhaps?"

"Just a friend." She leaned up and looked at him. "Jamie, being married should last forever, and the two people should have respect for each other. Sometimes that doesn't happen."

He regarded her for a moment. "Very often that doesn't happen, but people adjust and have workable lives. I know it can be done because, if you recall, my parents had such a relationship." He paused. "Is that what your friend was asking?"

"I think so," she said miserably. Was he telling her that he knew what marriage with Venetia would be like, that he was willing to make the "adjustments" his parents and others in the *ton* had made? She didn't want Jamie to have a life like that, so she tried again. "Jamie, there's something I really need to discuss with you."

He grinned crookedly at her. "I know, I know. You want to know when—and how—I plan to send Dee packing to Scotland." He sat up straight in the chair and crossed his legs. "I've already sent word to MacKenzie that we'll be there shortly. I have some business to take care of there anyway, so he can go along with me, and I'll keep an eye on him. Does that satisfy you?"

"The sooner the better," she said with feeling. "Dee needs to get out of Bath and discover there's something besides gaming and horse races."

"He'll grow out of it. I did, and I was worse than he's ever thought about being."

Callie laughed. "If your reputation is to be believed, you've grown worse instead of better."

"I foster that reputation very carefully, thank you," he said. "Do you realize how difficult it is to acquire a reputation of that caliber?"

She leaned forward and looked at him intently. "Why do you do that, Jamie? I know what kind of person you are, and Percy's told me what you've done with your estates and the mill houses. Why don't you show the world what kind of person you really are?"

His eyes widened in surprise, and he rumpled his hair with his fingers. "You always know where to hit me, Callie, and I suppose you're the only person in the world who could say that to me. I suppose, too, you're one of the few people who know the real James Williford." He stared at the flame of the candle while he thought. "You know what Father thought of me — nothing I did was ever up to his standards, so I finally decided to be what he thought I was. All of his friends, those trustees who attempt to run my life, think the same thing of me, and I refuse to give them the satisfaction of thinking I'm anything except a rake and a libertine." He looked at her and gave a rueful grin. "It doesn't make sense, does it?"

"It makes perfect sense to me, Jamie, because I know how your father treated you, but he's dead and gone. Don't you think you're just hurting yourself now?"

"I am, but I take something of a perverse pleasure in shocking people who prefer to know me through gossip. I really don't enjoy most of the things I do in London." He leaned forward and touched her hand. "Do you know what I like, Callie? I like to get out on the estates and talk to the tenants about what they're doing every day. I like to watch the hay being cut and the roofs being thatched. I like to smell the dirt and the sweat when the men are plowing." He paused and smiled. "Most of all, I like to go the mills and see the families living there in decent conditions." He leaned back in his chair where he could look at her. "Have you ever seen the houses that are clustered around some mills? London slums at their worst could never be that bad. Filth, poverty, terrible things." He

176

propped his feet on the little footstool by her bed and leaned farther back in his chair. "Did you know your father had faith in me, Callie? Something my father never had. Your father asked me if I would see to it that our workers were kept well housed and had a decent living. He even had enough faith in me so that he told MacKenzie that I would see to it, and by God, I have." He stopped, his face reddened slightly, and he gave an embarrassed chuckle. "I sound like a crusading Methodist, don't I?"

"No," she said quietly, "you sound like the Jamie I've always known. You've always taken care of other people. I suppose I was as bad as anyone. I listened to your father after you went away to school and believed some of the stories—I thought they were so outrageous they had to be true. I had forgotten what you were really like." She smiled at him. "I apologize, and I'm glad you came to Bath to see about Dee—or to find a bride. It gave us a chance to get reacquainted."

"I'm glad I came, too." He smiled at her. "As for the stories—I'm afraid most of them *were* true. I spent most of my time at school trying to be more outrageous than anyone else. Most of the time I succeeded." He paused as the hall clock chimed the half hour. "It's getting late. Have I answered your question about Dee? That was what you wanted to ask me, wasn't it?"

"Yes." She hesitated. "And to ask about your evening."

He shrugged. "As I said, it went well. Miss Bramley charmed everyone. The only dead part of the evening was when I went to get her and when I took her home. Miss Bramley doesn't seem to have much conversation except for chatter about clothes and society."

"No," Callie agreed, "that's most of Venetia's life." She stopped and traced a pattern on the counterpane. "She should fit right in with London society."

"Except I don't plan to spend much time in London anymore," Jamie said, with a strange tinge to his voice. "This stay in Bath—and perhaps your remarks—" he looked at her and smiled, "have made me realize that I need to stop a great deal of my frivolity."

"Just don't stop all of it," Callie said with a laugh, "or you wouldn't be my Jamie any more." She stopped abruptly as she realized what she had said, realized there was no way to amend it, but tried anyway. "That is, we all like you just the way you are."

"I'm glad. I've always been able to count on that from you, Callie." He turned toward the door. "Do you want me to snuff your candle before I leave? I can probably make it from here to the door without falling flat on my face."

"And if you don't?"

"Then I suppose the entire house will be in here. Perhaps Dee will even charge in waving that pistol again."

"Pistol? Whatever are you talking about, Jamie?"

He moved to the side of the bed. "Merely another interesting event in my life since I walked into this household. It's never dull around here, is it?" He waited until Callie had settled down in her bed and pulled the covers up under her chin. He regarded her for a long moment, and Callie wondered briefly if he was going to kiss her again. For an instant, she thought he was, but then he moved back a step. She wanted him to kiss her, she thought to her surprise. "Jamie," she said, searching for words.

178

"What?" He picked up the candle.

The moment had passed. "Good night."

He blew out the candle and murmured something in the dark before he made his way across the room and out the door, closing it softly behind him. Callie could have sworn that he had said "Sleep well, sweetheart," but that couldn't have been. Words like that were reserved for Venetia, who didn't want to hear them from Jamie.

It was a long time before Callie went to sleep.

Chapter Eleven

Callie slept in the next morning, not waking until the sun streamed through the windows. As she woke and stretched, she could hear the morning sounds of the house as the servants moved about. Outside, Bath was already bustling with people who had already been to take the waters, and Pulteney Street was full of the rattle of carriages and tradesmen traveling over the stones.

By the time Brewster had dressed her and she had gone downstairs, she found that Dee and Percy had gone out, Jamie had gone to see his Aunt Cavendish, and Aunt Mary was in a cleaning frenzy, ordering all the servants to polish everything in the house. Callie offered to help, but Aunt Mary told her that the best thing she could do was stay out of the way. With that in mind, she went to check on her drawings of Andrew so she could take one of them and do some preliminary color sketches.

She looked for a moment at the picture of Jamie propped against the wall, and then put it back. That one was work of a different kind to do, something she could work on later, after Jamie and Venetia had left Bath. She knew everything about him well enough to paint him from memory.

Turning to work, she took all the sketches she had made of Andrew and looked at them critically, again deciding definitely on the one of him sitting. She would add some color to the sketch and see if he liked it. It was by far the best, she thought.

She did a watercolor wash of the sketch and decided it would do very well. She would see Andrew, get his approval, then begin on the portrait. In preparation, she checked her paints and canvases. The coat Andrew had been wearing had been a deep green, and Callie discovered she had some green on hand, but not enough to do the entire coat. Since Aunt Mary was still creating chaos in the rest of the house, it would be a good time to walk down and have Mr. Newrich grind and mix some green for her.

Callie hadn't walked far, she had just passed over Pulteney Bridge, when she heard her name called. Turning, she saw Andrew coming up behind her. "How good to see you, Captain Sinclair," she said. "I was just on my way to get some paints for your portrait. I needed some green for your coat."

Andrew looked slightly alarmed. "Do you think the green suitable? Mama seemed to think I should wear blue velvet."

Callie surveyed him a moment, then shook her head. "No, I think the green superfine. Blue velvet is somewhat dated, and besides, I think you look much better in green. I think you'll agree when you see my sketch."

"If you really think so." Andrew appeared distracted. "Miss Stone, may I walk with you? I'd like to talk to you about Miss Bramley."

Callie sighed, but there was nothing she could do except say yes, so they walked slowly into Bath as Andrew talked and talked and talked about Venetia. Callie finally stopped listening to the words and just nodded and made sympathetic sounds here and there when he paused for breath. She was relieved when they reached Mr. Newrich's shop and she could talk about paints while Andrew waited. The time was too short, however, as they were back out on the street, paint in hand, all too soon, and Andrew was once again discussing his dear Miss Bramley. Callie lapsed again into reverie about her portraits while he talked and murmured "uuumm" at appropriate intervals.

"You will!" he exclaimed, seizing her hand. "Miss Stone, you've made me a happy man! I can't tell you how much this means to me."

Callie was going to ask what, but saw something familiar out of the corner of her eye and turned, Andrew still holding on to her hand. Jamie and Venetia were coming out of a ribbon and lace shop, not three feet from them. From their expressions, they had clearly heard Andrew. Jamie had a strange, shuttered expression, while Venetia's face registered shock that was slowly being replaced with rage.

After a moment, Venetia's recollected her manners and forced her countenance almost back to normal, although she was chalk-white and her mouth was a thin, angry line. Jamie stepped into the breach, cheerfully saying how delightful it was to see everyone out. Then polite murmurings were made all around, comments on the weather were exchanged, and Callie inquired after the health of Venetia's father and was told he was still ill but improving. After that, there was dead silence as the foursome stood awkwardly looking at each other.

Jamie again rescued them. "I'm afraid Miss Bramley and I must be going. We left her father only long enough for her to come buy some ribbon she needed, and she's promised to return and read to him. I hope we'll all meet again soon, perhaps at the Rooms, when Miss Bramley has the time to be out again."

"Wonderful idea," Callie said enthusiastically. "Very soon, I hope. Venetia, do come to see me." She smiled broadly at Venetia's glower, hooked her arm through Andrew's, and practically dragged him off down the street, chattering all the while as he looked back over his shoulder at Venetia and Jamie going the other way. As soon as they were near the Bridge, Callie stopped. There was something she had to know.

"Captain Sinclair," she said, facing him, "I'm afraid I really wasn't attending you earlier. Exactly what have I done to make you such a happy man?"

He looked confused. "You agreed that I should write a letter to Miss Bramley outlining my recent good fortune, the expectations of the title, and my plans: You thought I should offer marriage to her and agreed that you would talk to her about it. You agreed with me when I asked if she would accept." He looked at her accusingly. "You weren't paying attention? Then you don't think she will accept me?" He looked crestfallen and turned to look down Pulteney Street. "That was a very cruel thing to do, Miss Stone."

"I'm sorry I was distracted," Callie said, with a sigh. "As for whether she will accept you or not — you know her father has agreed to the match with Viscount Atwater. But I do promise you this, Captain Sinclair: if it's at all possible, I'll see Miss Bramley and tell her what

183

you've told me and what your expectations are."

"Soon?"

"I'll write her a note today, Captain, and talk to her as soon as she can see me. I'll ask if I might visit her this afternoon, if her father's health permits." Callie looked at his anxious face. "I'll let you know how it stands as soon as I know."

He was content with that, and offered to walk her home, but Callie politely refused. She wanted to be alone so she could think about things. Instead of going home, she went on down the street and into Sydney Gardens. She wandered about the gardens for a while, then sat down on a bench. In spite of Aunt Mary's strictures about sun on her skin, she took off her bonnet and turned her face up to feel the warm sun. She sat for a few minutes, enjoying the sensation before she felt guilty, hearing the inward voices of Brewster and Aunt Mary telling her to guard her complexion. She put her bonnet back on, then removed it and moved to the far end of the bench where there was shade. Over to the side of the Gardens, she saw some of the young ladies from school practicing their watercolors and sketching some of the trees and shrubbery. It didn't seem so long ago since Callie herself had been doing that. Yet in another way, it seemed an age. Not long ago Jamie had been only a memory from childhood and Venetia was sending giddy letters from Rome. For Callie, there had been no problems at all then.

Leaning back against a tree, she closed her eyes and let her mind wander. Actually, her life hadn't changed too much until lately; it had been much the same until Jamie had come to Bath. Since then, everything seemed to be a muddle. She needed time to think about the tangle of problems and what to do about them. Instead, her mind seemed to want to construct pictures of Jamie and how he looked when he smiled at her. With an effort, she made herself think about the problems with Dee, Jamie, Venetia, and Andrew Sinclair.

A family walked by her, the mother and father laughing as one child skipped along in front of them, and a chubby baby reached for leaves from overhanging limbs. Callie closed her eyes again, thinking about a family— she and Jamie walking along like that. Would their children look like him? Perhaps one of them would have that slightly crooked smile. Would they run and play as she and Jamie had done when they were children?

She forced herself to get up and walk. There was no point in torturing herself this way. She walked for a few minutes up the hill and then looked back down toward Bath. She leaned against a tree, feeling its rough bark against her back. "I'm in love with Jamie Williford," she whispered aloud, "and there's nothing I can do about it." That said, she felt better, although horribly empty.

Callie walked around the Gardens for a long while, thinking hard about Jamie and Venetia. She deliberately didn't let herself think about her feelings for Jamie. The thing that was most important to her was his happiness, and if he would be happy with Venetia, then that was what Callie wanted for him.

Finally, things sorted out somewhat in her mind, she made her way back toward Pulteney Street. She hadn't thought things through to her satisfaction, but had untangled them as best she could. After tonight at Bickell's, if her luck held as it had last night, Dee's problem would be solved. She would write Venetia and when they met, she would discuss both Captain Sinclair and Jamie. If

Venetia still planned to encourage Andrew, then there was nothing for it but to tell Jamie, straight out and bluntly. After that, if he still wanted to marry Venetia — Callie frowned as she worried about Jamie's reaction — if he still wanted to marry Venetia, then Callie would talk to Captain Sinclair. She felt Andrew was an honorable man and would do the right thing.

As Callie raised the knocker to the door, she realized she was ravenously hungry. "Mental exertion," she murmured to herself as John opened the door and she went inside. She glanced at the hall clock and discovered to her surprise that she had been gone longer than she thought — it was up into the afternoon. She left her bonnet in the hall and went to find something to eat.

Callie was in the middle of downing the better part of a platter of cold meat when Aunt Mary found her in the kitchen. "I'm glad to see your appetite has returned," Aunt Mary said approvingly. "There are two cream buns in the warmer."

"No," Callie said with a grin, "I've already eaten them."

"Good. You'll need your strength. Venetia's here and in a terrible state. You know how she gets at the slightest provocation, weeping, moaning, and whatnot. I tried to get her to tell me what had brought on such a fit of theatrics, but she refuses to speak to anyone except you."

"I didn't hear her come in," Callie said, wiping her fingers. "Why didn't John come get me?"

"She's been here for several minutes," Aunt Mary said, with a piercing look, "and I gave John strict instructions not to say anything to you. I wanted to speak to you before you saw her." Aunt Mary pulled out a chair and sat at the table beside Callie. "She said she had seen you at the ribbon shop and you were coming right home. She said you were with Captain Sinclair. Then she began wailing and tried to tell me some kind of gibberish about you and Captain Sinclair. She seems to think the two of you have a *tendre* for each other."

Callie's eyes widened. "That's ridiculous!"

"That's what I told her, but she wouldn't listen. She said I didn't know because you were trying to keep it a secret." Aunt Mary sniffed. "As if I didn't know everything going on in my own household! Sometimes I think that girl needs a good thump on the head. Perhaps lower and to the back." She looked straight at Callie. "However, as I have told you in the past, you could do worse than Captain Sinclair. He does seem a fine figure of a man."

"So he is, but that bird won't fly," Callie said with a laugh, "and don't play the matchmaker—you know it never works."

"True, but I keep trying. And I have my reasons." She couldn't suppress a long sigh. "You'd better see to Venetia."

Callie dropped a quick kiss on Aunt Mary's forehead and went to the library. She expected to find Venetia draped languidly over the sofa, sniffling into a dainty lace handkerchief. Instead, the Incomparable was huddled in a chair, rubbing at her cheeks with a large square, her face red and blotchy. She jumped up the second she saw Callie. "How could you?" she shrieked. "I thought you were my friend, and all the time you were a viper behind my back, stabbing me at the first opportunity. No wonder you promoted the match between Atwater and me!" She burst into a fresh flood of tears.

It took Callie a moment to sort through the idea of a viper stabbing anyone before she caught Venetia's words about Jamie. Before she could say anything, she had to calm Venetia. "Venetia, please." Callie reached out a hand to her.

"Don't touch me, you . . . you *vixen*."

Ignoring her theatrics, Callie grabbed her arms and sat her back down on the sofa, then sat beside her. "Venetia, hush that this moment," she said sharply, resisting the urge to follow Aunt Mary's advice and give the girl a smart thump. "I want you to stop crying and tell me what's bothering you."

"You ask me that — you, who've stolen my life from me!" Venetia buried her face in the square and Callie let her be for a moment. At least the wailing was muffled. It was fully five minutes before Venetia wiped her eyes and nose with the crumpled, wet square and turned with red-rimmed eyes to look accusingly at Callie.

"Don't say anything unless you make sense," Callie warned her. "I can't listen to you when you're hysterical." Callie started to touch her hand, but thought the better of it and simply waited for Venetia to speak.

"It's you and Andrew," Venetia said. "No, don't try to deny it, Callie, I saw and heard you today. I had wondered why you would be promoting a match between me and Atwater, and now I know it was because you wanted Andrew all to yourself. I'm telling you now that you can't have him. I love Andrew, and no matter what it takes, I'm going to be with him."

"*Promoting* the match? Venetia, has your mind turned to mush? I never did any such thing! As a matter of fact, I've never thought the two of you would suit."

"You've merely forgotten," Venetia said firmly. "I recall distinctly that you introduced the two of us. If that's not promoting a match, I don't know what is."

"I introduced the two of you because that was good manners," Callie pointed out. "However, that's immaterial right now. If you still want Captain Sinclair, what about Ja . . . Atwater?" Callie was bewildered by this outburst. "I thought you had decided that love was secondary and that you and Atwater would be a good match."

Venetia mopped at her eyes again, making them even redder, if it was possible. "Papa says it's a good match, and I agreed with him. Mama *insists* that I marry Atwater. I even thought for a while that I could go through with it. I thought I could marry him and it would be enough as long as I had a house in London and all the clothes he could buy for me." She turned to Callie. "But I can't, I just *can't* marry him, Callie. I love Andrew. I really do." There was a long pause before she began to wail again. "And now *you've* got him." She buried her face in the square again.

Callie leaned back against the sofa to try to think while Venetia cried. After a few moments, she straightened and shook Venetia. "Listen to me, Venetia. Stop that caterwauling." She spoke sharply, and waited for the crying to stop. When the noise had subsided to mere sniffles, she went on. "Venetia, Jamie's in love with you. You can't play fast and loose with people this way. Since you've told him you'll marry him, you can't just cry off and decide Andrew is the one you prefer. Don't you think Jamie deserves some consideration?"

"I don't care. I've always loved Andrew, Callie. You know that." She looked at Callie through swollen eyes. "That's why I can't understand why you'd take him from me."

"I didn't take him from you. I don't care for Andrew

189

at all, and if you were rational, you'd know that."

"James said you had a *tendre* for Andrew." The tone was accusatory. "He said you were thinking about marriage."

"What!" She looked incredulously at Venetia while Venetia recounted a conversation with Jamie. Then Callie closed her eyes for a moment while several remarks Jamie had made fell into place. "Venetia, I can assure you that I have never cared for Andrew except as a friend," she said, "and what Jamie told you about the sketches being placed out where I could see them was true." She paused before plunging into the next subject since this would probably seal Jamie's heartbreak. But, she told herself, Venetia had to know — she would find out sooner or later. "Captain Sinclair's expectations have increased, Venetia. His cousin died unexpectedly, and his uncle is ill as well. Captain Sinclair believes he will soon be Lord Easton and more than comfortable." She held up a hand to stop Venetia from speaking. "No, let me finish. The sketches were around because Captain Sinclair has asked me to do his portrait, something that will do credit to his new position. I, as usual, did several sketches to decide on a final pose. You know how I work." She sat on the edge of the sofa so she could look full at Venetia. "What you heard outside the ribbon shop was Captain Sinclair saying he was delighted that I had agreed to see you and tell you about his expectations." Callie paused, then forced herself to go on. She didn't want to do this to Jamie. "Captain Sinclair is still in love with you," she said slowly.

Venetia threw her arms around Callie. "I knew it! Oh, my dear Andrew! Callie, you must arrange it so that I can see Andrew."

"No." Callie already felt like a traitor. She wouldn't do

190

anything else to spoil Jamie's happiness. "I'll tell him what I've told you, and if he wants to write you, or you him, that's your business. I've done all I'm going to."

Venetia leaned back and closed her swollen eyes, a beatific smile on her face. "Lady Easton . . . Doesn't it sound wonderful, Callie?"

"Perhaps you should wait until the present Lord Easton dies," Callie said tartly. "If I recall correctly, you said much the same words when you were planning on being Lady Atwater." She paused. "Venetia, you *must* think about Jamie. After all, he does care for you, and this is going to hurt him terribly."

"Papa told me that no one ever died from a broken heart." Venetia turned pale. "Papa! Do you think he will like Andrew any better since his expectations have increased?" She put her hands over her face. "I don't think he likes Andrew very much."

Callie couldn't think anymore. "Venetia, why don't you just do nothing for a few days? Perhaps by then Captain Sinclair will know about his inheritance and you'll have some time to decide how to cry off with Atwater. I don't want him to be hurt, Venetia."

Venetia looked sharply at her. "Why should you care, Callie? I didn't think you held Atwater in very high regard."

Callie fought down a blush, but she couldn't look straight at Venetia. "We're old friends. I don't want him hurt." She put her fingers to her head. It was beginning to ache, a dull hurt that began right behind her eyes. "Please, just don't do anything for a few days, Venetia."

"But I want to see Andrew."

"I promise I'll talk to him at the earliest opportunity. Don't do anything until I talk to him."

"Are you well, Callie? You look so pale." Venetia reached over and touched Callie's forehead. "You're not hot."

"Just a slight headache." In truth, her head was beginning to throb in earnest.

"I'm going to leave so you can get some rest." Venetia stood up. "Don't worry about a thing."

"You won't try to reach Andrew? You won't do anything?"

"Don't worry about a thing," Venetia repeated as she picked up her reticule and opened the door. "Good-bye, and thank you." She blew Callie a kiss as she closed the door behind her.

Callie leaned back, closed her eyes, located the center of the throbbing pain behind her eyes, and moaned, "Oh, Lord." After a few moments when things didn't get any better, she took Venetia's advice and went upstairs to bed.

Chapter Twelve

It was late afternoon when Callie awoke to Dee shaking her. "What time do you want to leave tonight?" he asked, before she was fully awake.

"Tonight?" She was trying to clear her head. There was still a dull ache behind her eyes. "What's going on tonight?"

"Good Lord, don't you remember?" he asked impatiently. "We're going to Bickell's. I thought we should get there about nine or so. Aunt Mary's going out again, so we don't have to come up with a reason for being out of the house."

Callie shut her eyes. "Maybe not a reason for leaving, but we'll have to explain ourselves for coming in late."

"We'll think of something," Dee said, heading for the door. "You be ready a little before nine — I want you sharp for tonight." He grinned at her. "After all, tonight's the night you save the family fortunes." He laughed as he went out.

Callie groaned as she sat up in bed and shoved her hair back from her face. It wasn't five minutes until Brewster, bless her, brought in a tray with something to eat and, most important, some hot, strong tea. "I saw Mr. DeQunicey leaving, so I thought you might be awake." Her glance took in Callie's wan face. "I believe you need this."

"I certainly do," Callie agreed, sipping the tea. "Have I ever told you that you're a jewel, Brewster?"

All she got in reply was a *"humpf,"* but Callie saw a pleased smile as Brewster closed the door behind her. Contentedly, Callie poured herself some more tea, buttered a slice of newly baked bread, and leaned back to savor the taste. She refused to think about anything for at least fifteen minutes except the smell and taste of the tea, bread, and fruit Brewster had brought in.

When she finished, she felt much better. The headache was still a tiny, nagging pinpoint behind her eyes, but perhaps it would go away later. If tonight at Bickell's went as well as last night, she could clear Dee's debts, and he had promised her he would never get under the hatches again. As for Venetia and Jamie, that would have to wait. Right now, Callie decided, she simply wasn't up to doing anything about it. Since she didn't know what to do anyway, there wasn't any point in worrying about it until she had gotten Dee's problem out of the way. She went to her clothespress and finally decided on a dark green gown trimmed with white lace and black ribbons: sedate, authoritative, and still fashionable. That decided, she went downstairs to engage in a probing conversation to find out exactly when Aunt Mary would be coming home. Perhaps her luck had changed—things were falling into place.

"My God, Callie, of all the rotten luck," Dee said into

the silence as they went home. It was after one in the morning, and although Dee had pressed her to stay at Bickell's and play, she had quit and asked him to take her home. "If you'd stayed, your luck would have turned for the better, I know it. *Nobody* could have that much bad luck."

"I did," Callie said dejectedly, "and now I've not only lost what we won last night, but Bickell has all your vowels, and all of mine promising my allowance for the next quarter. I don't know how I could have played so badly."

"Don't fret yourself," Percy said. "Cardsharps."

"Easy enough for you to say," Dee muttered under his breath.

They had reached the door and went in quietly. Dee and Percy started up the steps to their rooms, but Callie stopped them. "Let's go to the library for a few minutes."

Once there, she closed the door behind them and lit some candles. "What do you mean, 'cardsharps,' Percy?"

"Well, don't get so offended. I told you that M'liss had been in Paris learning the trade. I thought you knew what I meant."

"I thought you meant she'd been learning how to run a gambling house," Callie said, slumping into a chair.

"Well, what do you think that involves? She was learning how to spot an easy mark — not that you're one, by any means," he added hastily. "I suppose she was also learning how to let customers win so they'll return and play deeper next time, and it's only reasonable to expect that she learned how to cheat at cards."

"I didn't even think of anyone cheating," Callie said, "and I suppose I was an easy mark. One look at me and M'liss knew that I was as green as a goose."

Dee walked over and stirred the embers in the fireplace. "All this gnashing of teeth is rather immaterial at this point, isn't it? The fact is that we were royally taken and now we have to come up with some other way to pay the piper. What are we going to do?"

There was a long, tense silence. Percy finally stood up. "Perhaps I should go on to bed so the two of you can talk. My offer to lend you the money still stands, if you want it." There was an awkward pause. "Since you won't let me help you, then my advice is still the same: talk to James."

"I don't want to ask Jamie to bail us out, Percy, although I don't know what else to do." She held up a hand to stop him from saying anything else. "Thank you for your generous offer, but we can't." She smiled at him softly. "Thank you for being such a friend, Percy. I'll always be grateful to you for offering."

"I mean it," he said gruffly. "All you have to do is say the word. Lord, I spent more than that on boarding my horseflesh last year." He looked from one of them to the other. "I still say you should discuss this with James. He's got your best interests at heart, you know, both as your guardian and as a friend. You should at least give him the opportunity to help." He walked over to the door and paused before he went out. "James has a good heart, he really does." He left and they heard the boards creak as he went softly up the stairs to his room.

Dee looked at Callie with a rueful smile. "It's funny. Six months ago, I despised James without knowing him, and I despised everything people like Percy stood for. Now I see I was the shallow one. I suppose I've changed."

"I think it's called growing up," Callie said, with as much of a grin as she could manage. "Percy means well, and he's right — Jamie will do everything he can for us."

"Yes, Percy's right—James does have a good heart," Dee said, sitting down across from Callie.

"He does, but I still don't want to ask him for help, Dee. There's got to be some other way."

"There isn't," Dee said bluntly. "I've thought about it a dozen different ways from Sunday, and there's nothing else to be done. There's no reason I need to mention you in this mess, though. I'll just tell James that I went to Bickell's again and got taken." He made a face, and Callie knew how much an admission like that would cost him. "He'll ring a peal over me," Dee continued, "but he'll pay it off. Then he'll probably pack me off to Scotland, but I was going anyway. Actually," he said, with a flash of a grin, "I've been looking forward to making an impression in the land of kilts and red-haired girls."

"Don't try to cozen me," Callie said, "and, furthermore, don't think for one minute I'm going to let you take all the blame. Here I have been ranting at you about your gambling, and how do I try to help you pay off your debts?" She grimaced and gave Dee a rueful grin. "The thing that really galls me is being taken in by that sweet, simpering masquerade of a little girl. I should have known better."

Dee grinned back at her. "M'liss, the cardsharp . . . do you know that both James and Percy sized her up in one glance and told me exactly what she was? James, in particular, told me to watch out. I thought she was a sweet girl and James just didn't know her."

Callie sighed and put her hand to her head. "Well, neither of us listened to what we were told, and now we can't cry over spilled milk. What do you think of the idea of writing Angus MacKenzie?"

"Good Lord, Callie, are you out of your mind! I'd

rather face a dozen dragons than Angus MacKenzie."

She put both hands over her face and pressed against her eyes. Her head was hurting again. "All right. We'll tell Jamie, but let me do it."

Dee shook his head. "No, if you don't want me to talk to him alone, then we do it together."

"Dee, there's something you don't know." Callie paused. "Jamie's going to be hurt anyway. Venetia came to see me and she'll probably cry off because she still says she's in love with Andrew. That'll be a bitter thing for a proud man like Jamie."

"I'm sure it will be," Dee said with sarcasm. "He'll probably be so crushed that he'll dance a jig in the middle of the Pump Room." Dee stood and walked to the window. "We might as well go to bed."

"What do you mean, Jamie will be happy enough to dance? He's in love with Venetia; Percy told me so."

Dee turned and looked at her in the shadowy candlelight. "Callie, I may be a green 'un in a thousand ways, but from what little I've been around James and Venetia, I can see that he doesn't care a thing for her. Actually, I think it took him about five minutes to discover what a silly bubblehead she is."

"You're wrong, Dee. He's in love with her, I know it; and I can't stand the thought of him being hurt. In this situation, either way he loses. If Venetia cries off, he'll be hurt, but if they marry, she vows to keep up her friendship with Andrew Sinclair, so Jamie will be hurt. He can't win."

"He'll win if he gets rid of Venetia's scheming pack of relatives. Personally, I wouldn't have the girl on a gold-plated stick." He came over and held out a hand for her. "Let's go to bed. Tomorrow we'll get together."

Callie rose to her feet and they went upstairs. "Dee, I still think you're wrong," she said, her voice troubled. "He does care for Venetia."

"Have it your way," he said absently. "We can't do much about his affairs of the heart, anyway. I'll see you tomorrow." They stopped in front of her door and he suddenly leaned over and gave her a kiss on the cheek. "Glad you're my sister, Callie," he said in a hurry, then went on down the hall. Callie smiled after him and went into her room.

She wearily climbed into bed, thinking she would go to sleep instantly and feel better tomorrow. She sat up in the bed, propped up against the pillows, watching the candle flame flicker shadows on the wall as she thought. No matter how she thought about it, she always came up with the same answer: she was going to have to tell Jamie about the losses at Bickell's and take the consequences, and she was going to have to tell Jamie about Venetia and Andrew. Much as she dreaded doing the first, the second was worse. How do you tell a man that the woman he loves doesn't care for him? Callie knew her heart would break if she had to see him hurt.

She blew out the candle and lay there in the dark, listening and thinking. Finally, she sat up again, lit a fresh candle from the drawer, and gave up on the idea of sleeping. "Oh, Jamie, what a mess," she murmured as she leaned back against her pillows and closed her eyes.

A heavy thump followed by a muffled curse woke her up early. The first light of a gray day was coming in through the window where the curtains hadn't been closed completely. The candle had burned down into a puddle of wax and made strange shapes on the walls as it seemed to go out, then revive. The house was quiet in the early morning stillness, and Callie decided she had dreamed the noise. She was awake now, so she got out of bed, stretched, then poured some water from the pitcher without looking at herself in the mirror. That reflection was the last thing she wanted to see. The water was cool and invigorating as she splashed her face. To her surprise, she was ravenous, so she smoothed her hair, put on her dressing gown, and slipped softly out into the hall.

She paused and looked at the doors. She must have dreamed the sound she had heard as no one seemed to be up, so she tiptoed to the stairs and went down to the kitchen. John was nowhere to be seen, but he had already built a fire there. The warmth felt good in the morning chill. Callie was rummaging around for some chocolate and a pot when John came in from outside. Jamie was with him, dressed for riding. They looked at Callie in surprise as she stood there in her dressing gown holding a pot in one hand.

"Could I get something for you, Miss Stone?" John asked, more formally than usual, averting his eyes from her dressing gown and concentrating on a point in the center of the cupboard.

Callie waved the pot in his general direction. "No, I woke up early and wanted some chocolate."

"If you'll sit here a moment, I'll start a fire in the morning room and you can have your chocolate there. Meg'll be right in to fix it."

"No need," Jamie said authoritatively. "John, why don't you take a few extra minutes this morning? I'm sure Miss Stone can make some chocolate for the two of us." He looked at John. "Or would you like to join us?"

John was horrified at the suggestion and left, saying

he needed to attend to things in the rest of the house. Callie laughed as she got the chocolate out. "You shouldn't offend John's sense of propriety like that, Jamie. You'll send him into apoplexy. Do you want sugar in your chocolate?"

"Any way," he said absently, sitting down and watching her.

"I have Meg put this in mine," she said, getting down a canister of pounded sugar with a bit of vanilla bean in it for flavoring.

In minutes they were sitting at the kitchen table in front of the fire, sipping chocolate. Jamie seemed tense and preoccupied, so Callie said nothing. Jamie finished his chocolate and got up. "I'm going out for a ride," he said abruptly. "I don't know when I'll be back."

"What's wrong, Jamie?"

"Nothing." He shook his head. "I'll sort it out." He looked over at her sitting at the table and smiled. "Nice, isn't it?" At her puzzled look, he explained. "The two of us, sitting at the kitchen table in the morning, drinking chocolate."

She smiled back. "Like when we were children and used to slip into the kitchen so cook would give us cookies and milk."

"Yes. Those were good times then, and we didn't even know it." He smiled at her and sat down again. "I heard you rattling around your room last night late. Is something bothering you?" He touched her hand briefly.

For a moment Callie thought about the agreement she and Dee had to tell Jamie together, but then she decided the opportunity was too perfect to pass by. Where else could she engage Jamie in a conversation where there were just the two of them? She hesitated for a mo-

201

ment, then took a deep breath and began. "Jamie, there's something I have to tell you."

"Yes?" He leaned toward her, and the distance between them was small. He smiled at her, that slightly lopsided smile she loved to watch, and she had to force herself not to look at him.

"You know I've been worried about Dee," she began, but he interrupted her.

"I know that, Callie, and I told you I'd take care of it. I've talked to him, and he promised me that he wouldn't be gambling any more—at least, not more than his pockets could handle." He leaned back in his chair and regarded her. "Is that all that's bothering you? I had imagined there was something more."

Callie bit her lip. How would she ever be able to tell him about Venetia? She still hadn't managed to tell him about her part in Dee's predicament. She tried again. "There is—something more, I mean, but right now I want to talk to you about Dee." She held up a hand to stop him from saying anything. "Dee owed a good bit to Bickell," she said, not looking at him, "and he didn't want to ask you for the money to pay gambling debts."

"I told him I would take care of everything."

"I know, but I agreed with Dee. It just didn't seem right to ask you to take care of something that wasn't your responsibility, and we didn't want to do it."

He touched the back of her hand. "Did it ever occur to you that I like having the two of you as a responsibility? Actually, I don't think of it as a responsibility at all—it's more of something I want to do for people I care about."

Callie closed her eyes to keep tears from falling. "Please, Jamie, don't say anything else until I can tell you this. It's difficult enough for me." At his nod, she continued, concentrating on the edge of her chocolate cup and speaking in slow, embarrassed tones until she had told him everything. She didn't spare herself at all. When she finished, he was very quiet, then he reached over and touched her face with his fingertips. She hadn't realized she was crying.

"It's all right, sweet. You were trying to do what you thought was best. I think it was a wonderful thing for you to do."

"But Jamie, look what I did! I lost Dee's money and mine, too."

Jamie reached over and took her in his arms. "What you did was try to help your brother, and I think it was a magnificent thing for you to do. Don't worry about Bickell, I'll see him this afternoon and take care of everything." Callie put her head against his shoulder. It felt so good for him to hold her, so *right*. "It's all right, sweetheart," he murmured against her hair.

Callie sat up straight and looked at him. "Jamie, what would we do without you?" she asked with a wavering smile.

"I don't ever want you to . . ." He stopped himself. He had almost told her that he never wanted her to be without him. Instead, he pulled back and smiled rather formally at her. "I don't ever want you to think you can't come to me with a problem."

"I won't, I promise." She mopped at her eyes with the sleeve of her dressing gown, and he spent a moment searching for his handkerchief, glad when he didn't have to look at her and see the expression in her eyes. All too soon he had to look at her again and hand her his handkerchief. "I believe you said there was something besides Dee that was bothering you," he prompted.

Callie looked back down at her cup. "I was going to talk to you about Venetia."

He leaned back in his chair and stretched his legs out. "Why that?" he asked sharply. "Don't tell me you think I'm in as much of a bramble as Dee!"

She closed her eyes briefly. "Yes, I think you are."

He stood up and his voice was abrupt. "I think I can manage on my own, but thank you for your concern."

"Jamie," she said, looking up at him pleadingly, "it's more than concern. You can't marry Venetia, you simply can't."

"And why not? She's presentable, she's accustomed to moving in society, she has a dozen other qualities that make her acceptable."

Callie listened carefully for other words, but there were none. Amazed, she stared at Jamie. "Don't you love her?"

"Love?" He laughed, a harsh, brittle sound. "Callie, you should know that love and marriage, especially in the *ton,* have very little to do with each other."

"You don't!" Callie said, jumping up and throwing her arms around Jamie. "You *don't* love her, and Percy said you did. So it's all right if she doesn't love you!"

He put his hands on her arms. "Callie, whatever are you talking about with all this gibberish about love?"

Callie stepped back. "She doesn't love you," she blurted out.

He moved away from her and picked up his gloves. "Of course she doesn't," he said. "Venetia doesn't care two pins for me, but then, I doubt she loves anything or anyone except herself."

"You know that and you still plan to marry her?"

204

He looked at her. "Of course. Do you think ordinary people are like the people in those novels you read? I don't mean to echo Aunt Mary, but you need to get your feet on the ground." He turned and put his hand on the door latch. "I don't think your Andrew will be so concerned about being romantic after the two of you are married."

"Andrew?" She stared at him. "Andrew? Venetia told me you had a notion about that. For your information, I have absolutely no intention of marrying Andrew. He wants to marry Venetia."

It was his turn to stare at her, then his lips twisted into something resembling a smile. "Does he, now?" he asked softly. "I thought he had fixed his affections on you after he discovered your regard for him."

"I've never cared for Andrew. All he ever wants to do is talk about is Venetia. I don't see what she sees in him at all."

Jamie laughed aloud. "That's precisely what she sees in him." Then he looked at Callie steadily. "Do you mean that — you don't care for him at all? Why were you drawing pictures of him?"

Callie rolled her eyes. "I happen to paint portraits. Since Andrew thinks he'll be the next Lord Easton, he wanted his portrait painted. His mother thinks it would be a good idea." She made a face at Jamie and he chuckled. "Those were preliminary sketches."

"How about that!" Jamie grabbed her by the waist and whirled the two of them around. Then he became serious and put her down. "Callie, promise me you won't do anything or go anywhere until I return. I have some things to do this morning and I may not be back for a while."

She hesitated to ask him again. "You'll see about Bickell?"

"Yes. Don't worry about it." He laughed. "Don't ever worry about anything ever again. I'm not going to."

She hesitated again, not able to read his mood. "Jamie, about Venetia—I won't say anything else right now, but we do need to talk later." She looked at him and he had a strange expression on his face. "I'd never want to hurt you, you know that."

"I know that." His mood changed again. "If Mother or Aunt Cavendish stops by, tell her I'll be back later." He went outside, and Callie could hear him calling for the groom to bring his horse. In a moment, she heard him ride away, the horse's hooves clattering.

Something was bothering him greatly, she knew, and it was probably his engagement to Venetia. Perhaps he knew deep down how unsuited they were. Callie had always been able to know when he was thinking about a problem. When they were children, Jamie always had one way of working his problems out—he had gotten on his horse and ridden for miles, thinking. She leaned against the door and smiled, remembering him. When he returned from those rides, he had always had a solution. Perhaps this time would be the same.

Chapter Thirteen

To Callie's surprise, when Dee came downstairs and she told him she had already talked to Jamie, he wasn't at all angry. In fact, she thought, "relieved" might be the best word to describe him. "Did James rant and rave?" he asked.

"Not at all. He was really very sweet about it."

Dee stared at her. "Sweet? Callie, this is James Williford we're discussing. 'Sweet' is hardly a term I'd use."

"Well, I would," she answered. "Jamie happens to be a very sweet person. He's caring, considerate, and helpful. Dee, he's become the most responsible person alive. I only wish his father could see him now."

Dee was looking at her, amazed. "Good God, Callie, it almost sounds as if . . ." He stopped and peered at her closely. "You are, you really are. Good God, Callie, you're in *love* with him!"

Callie felt her face go red, and she couldn't look at Dee. She started to deny it, but there was no use. "Don't say anything, Dee, please." There were tears behind her eyes. "Jamie doesn't care about me, and I don't want to say or do anything that would make him feel awkward around me."

"Poor girl," Dee said, patting her hand, "but you underestimate yourself. James couldn't do any better than you."

"The daughter of a woolen merchant?" she asked bitterly. "When he could have his pick of any woman in the *ton*?"

"You're doing him a disservice, Callie . . . James knows what a fine man Father was; your background wouldn't make a difference to him."

Callie shook her head. "It would to everyone else in the *ton*. Besides," she said with an attempt to control her voice, "nothing is going to happen between Jamie and me, so I don't ever want him to know that I care. We can always be friends."

"Callie," Dee began, but was stopped as the front door opened and Aunt Mary walked in, followed by a very distinguished gentleman who was elegantly dressed in dark green and buff.

"I'm quite surprised to see the two of you up," she said briskly. "I had fully expected to find both of you abed. Come, I have something to tell you." She shepherded the two of them and the gentleman with her into the library. "First," she said, taking off her bonnet, "allow me to introduce Henry Waring, Lord Easton."

Callie gaped. "Lord Easton? Andrew's relative?"

Lord Easton nodded. "Andrew Sinclair? Yes, my heir. Mary told me you were acquainted."

Callie looked at him from head to toe. He certainly looked fit enough. "I'm sorry, I thought you were quite ill. That is, Andrew thought . . . Andrew said that . . ." She gave up and looked at Aunt Mary, who was standing beside Lord Easton, looking very smug.

"Henry was ill and in shock. He came to Bath to try to

regain his health after his son's funeral. We met the day he arrived in Bath and resumed our acquaintance." She blushed and looked up adoringly at Lord Easton. "Henry and I were quite well acquainted at one time, long ago, before I married Mr. Elliot."

"Actually, we were engaged," Lord Easton said, patting Aunt Mary's hand, "and when we met all these years later, we knew things hadn't changed at all."

Aunt Mary blushed like a schoolgirl. "What Henry means to say is that we've become engaged again. His health isn't the best, and what with the shocks he's had to endure lately, he needs someone to look after him."

"Now, Mary, you know I'm not looking for a nurse-maid. I could hire someone to do that. You know the reason I want to marry you." They stood and looked at each other while Dee and Callie stared first at the two of them and then at each other in amazement.

"You're getting married?" Dee finally asked.

"Yes," Aunt Mary exclaimed, "isn't it the most wonderful thing? It was just like one of those terrible books Callie always has around. Henry and I simply looked at one another and the years dropped away. It was as if we were both twenty again."

"You still look as lovely as you did then," Lord Easton said gallantly, between coughs.

Aunt Mary promptly sat him down and rang for tea, fussing over him like a mother hen.

"Good heavens," Callie said suddenly, collapsing into the nearest chair. "I believe Andrew will be surprised."

Lord Easton chuckled. "I suppose he will be, especially since his mama expects me to stick my spoon in the wall momentarily. I thought I was going to for a while, but my Mary has given me a new life." He coughed while

209

Aunt Mary plumped a pillow and put it behind him, then he waited while she stirred sugar and cream into his tea. Aunt Mary, Callie noted, was in her element.

"I had meant to call on Andrew," Lord Easton continued, "but I met Mary first, and haven't had time. I don't think the fact that I plan to be around for a few years more will bother Andrew as much as it will his mother. From what I know, he's all right, although he depends too much on his mother's advice. He's still my heir, though, and I plan to see to it that he'll be well off. He seems like a good boy, although a trifle unimaginative."

"True," Callie agreed, watching Aunt Mary bustle around. "Aunt Mary, when do the two of you plan to get married?"

Aunt Mary blushed and looked at Lord Easton. "At our age, we decided we shouldn't wait, especially since we've known each other for more than half a lifetime." There was a delicate pause. "We would expect the two of you to live with us, of course."

"Aunt Mary, we couldn't do that . . ." Callie began, but was stopped when both Lord Easton and Aunt Mary began talking together. Dee came to stand behind her and put his hands on her shoulders. "Now we have not one, but two supervisors in the family," he said with a grin. "We won't have the chance of a snowball in July with both of them seeing to us."

"Sensible boy," Aunt Mary said, looking with satisfaction at Dee.

They spent the next half hour talking, listening to tales that Aunt Mary and her Henry had to tell of their early engagement and the quarrel that had separated them. He had married many years later, but it was not a happy marriage. It was obvious to both Dee and Callie that the two of them were very much in love. By the time Lord Easton took his leave, both Callie and Dee very much approved of him and the match. As the door closed behind Lord Easton, Aunt Mary smiled beatifically at them and went upstairs, singing a song.

"Well, wonders fill the earth," Dee said, as they watched her disappear around the bend in the stairs. "She didn't even ask whether or not we had eaten breakfast."

"What are we going to do about living with them? I don't want to leave Bath."

Dee glanced at her. "Good Lord, Callie, don't worry about it. It'll work itself out."

"That's easy enough for you to say — you'll be in Scotland, and, if I recall correctly, you'll be keeping company with all those pretty red-haired lassies. I'll be the one who'll have to move."

"Won't hurt you," Dee said jauntily. "I'm going out. If you see Percy, tell him to meet me at Mollands in Milsom Street around three." He started out the door, then turned and gave Callie a quick kiss on the cheek. "Everything will work out all right, big sister. Wait and see." Before she could think of a tart reply, he was gone.

"I repeat — that's easy enough for you to say," she said to the closed door, then went to find John and give him Dee's message in case she didn't see Percy.

Aunt Mary went out again to visit friends — no doubt to share her news — still singing under her breath, and Callie tried to busy herself with her portraits. She couldn't do it, and in disgust spent the better part of an hour cleaning her brushes and paint containers. Finally, she had everything arranged neatly in the cupboard she used to store her supplies. Jamie hadn't returned, she had promised not to talk to Venetia yet, and there was nothing more she wanted to do with her portraits. Restless, she decided to go for a walk in Sydney Gardens. It was always a good place to sit and think.

She had changed into a sprigged dress and a shawl and was just getting ready to go out when John announced a visitor. Going into the small drawing room, she was surprised to see Mr. Bickell there waiting for her.

He sat down and declined tea, then got right to the point. "I know you and your brother are good for your vowels, Miss Stone, but I'm somewhat short of ready cash right now, so I need to collect. I realize you might not have that much money around the house, so I'm willing to wait until tomorrow morning."

Callie sat and listened to him, very pale. "This is rather sudden, Mr. Bickell."

"You can't deny you owe me, Miss Stone."

She swallowed her anger and kept her voice level. "No, I do not deny it, Mr. Bickell. I'll settle both my debts and Dee's as soon as possible. I'll discuss it with Viscount Atwater this evening, and I'm sure it will be settled by tomorrow morning."

"Atwater? What does he have to do with it?" Bickell demanded, his florid face paling. "This is just between the two of us, Miss Stone, or, if you want to include your brother, the three of us."

There was a sound at the door while Bickell was speaking and Jamie walked in, still wearing his riding clothes, his boots covered with dust. He threw his gloves onto a chair and leaned back against a table. "Actually, Bickell, anything that concerns Miss Stone and her brother is a concern of mine. In case you don't know, they're my wards. In that capacity, I treat their problems as my own.

212

Now just what do you want?" Callie had never heard Jamie speak so. His face was set and white, his voice hard and cold.

Bickell was at his most urbane. "I merely came to discuss a small matter with Miss Stone. It's of no importance. Now if you'll excuse me . . ." He stood and picked up his hat, but Jamie put a hand on his arm.

"Am I correct in assuming that you've come to Miss Stone demanding payment for the debts she incurred last night? If so, Bickell, I suggest you apologize to the lady and then you and I will discuss this." Jamie's knuckles were white on Bickell's arm.

"Now see here," Bickell blustered, "this is merely a business discussion."

"Exactly," Jamie said, his voice low. He did not take his hand from Bickell's arm. "And since it is, perhaps you wish to apologize to Miss Stone now before I forget this is a discussion."

Bickell paled and turned to Callie. "My apologies, Miss Stone. I'm sorry I bothered you with this triviality. I should have known better."

"Mr. Bickell," Callie began, but Jamie interrupted her, not taking his eyes from Bickell. "Callie, perhaps you could leave Mr. Bickell and me alone for a few minutes to continue this discussion. I have some things I'd like to say to him." Jamie's voice was still icy, and he hadn't let go of Bickell's arm. Callie started to argue with him, but stopped herself. "I'll be in the library," she said. "I'd like to talk to you as soon as possible."

There was no answer, so she went on out the door, pulling it shut behind her. John was standing in the hall, staring. "Don't you have anything to do, John?" Callie asked sharply, then waited until he had disappeared before dashing back to the drawing room door and putting her ear to the panel. Aware of a movement next to her, she glanced up to find John standing there.

"Perhaps I should be ready in case the Viscount needs some help," John whispered hoarsely, moving to the other side of the door. "I can hold my own if needs be." Callie meant to send him packing to some other part of the house, but thought the better of it as Jamie and Bickell started talking loud enough to hear. She and John got close to the door and listened intently.

"The Viscount's telling 'im right proper," John whispered as they heard Jamie threaten to turn Bickell in for running an illegal house. In a moment, Jamie suggested Bickell take M'liss and stay in Paris for a few months. There was only an answering murmur from Bickell. John stood up, and he and Callie moved away from the door. "No point in us staying close," John observed, glancing at the door. "The Viscount's takin' right good care of things, as best as I can tell. He don't need any help from us."

"No," Callie agreed, "he certainly doesn't. It all seems to be the other way around." She went on to the library to wait for Jamie, trying to frame what she could say to him. She couldn't come up with very much except a fervent "Thank you," and that didn't seem to be enough.

Jamie came in the door while she was looking out the window. "Did you want to see me?" he asked. "I'm sorry Bickell came here to bother you. I had stopped by his house. I had thought to settle things this morning, but I had some other things to do first and missed him." He sat down in a chair and stretched out his legs. "He didn't upset you, did he?"

Callie walked over and sat down in the chair next to

214

his. "No, not really. I felt embarrassed that he would come here, but no one saw him except the two of us and John. John will never tell."

"No, and Bickell won't be back," Jamie said shortly. "Did you have something else you wanted to talk about?" There was a pause.

"I just wanted to thank you." Callie couldn't look at him.

He took her hand in his. "There's no need for that. I said your problems were mine, and that's how I feel." He sat up straight. "Do you think I could convince the cook to send me something to eat? I've been so busy today, I haven't stopped for anything."

Callie jumped from her chair and pulled the bell-rope. "Why didn't you say something? You shouldn't miss meals."

"Aunt Mary has rubbed off on you," Jamie said, grinning. He turned the conversation to generalities until a tray had been brought in and he had eaten. Callie joined him in a cup of tea after John had removed the tray. "Now," Jamie said, "I do have a surprise for you." He finished his tea and put the cup down.

"Must you take forever?" Callie asked. "Tell me."

He chuckled. "Always the impatient one, aren't you? Very well — I've been busy all day, as I told you. I went to visit Captain Sinclair this morning."

"Oh, Jamie, I forgot to tell you about Lord Easton!" she exclaimed, but he stopped her. "Later. Let me get this out of the way first." He paused and looked solemnly at her. "Are you sure you don't care for Captain Sinclair?"

"I'm sure . . . why?"

"Because I went to see him and told him that I felt he should marry Venetia Bramley. Then I went to Miss

215

Bramley and told her I thought she should marry Captain Sinclair. Then I got the two of them together at Aunt Cavendish's for a meeting. Needless to say, Miss Bramley and I are no longer engaged." He accepted the refilled teacup Callie handed him and took a sip. "Also, needless to say, I am delighted."

"Are you, Jamie? Really? You're not hurt because Venetia doesn't love you?"

"I always knew Venetia didn't love me, you goose. And no, I'm not at all hurt. What I am is overjoyed. Venetia Bramley, bless her mercenary little soul, is a complete featherhead." He reached for her hand. "And now, there is one other thing I want to do."

There was a commotion in the hall outside, and Callie glanced up just as Dee dashed into the room. "John said the two of you were in here," he said in a rush. "Do you know what I just heard? Bickell was in Milson Street heading for home. He told me he and M'liss were planning on going to Paris for a few months. It seems M'liss missed all those Frenchies, if you can believe that." He stood and looked from one of them to the other. "Have I interrupted something?"

"Not at all," Jamie said. "Sit down and join us. Callie and I were just getting ready to discuss your trip to Scotland."

Dee sat down. "Percy's going with me, you know."

"No, I didn't know that," Jamie said. "What brought that on?"

"We've become good friends. I think he wants to save me from boredom in Scotland."

"He probably plans to save you from the clutches of all those red-haired lassies you're planning to meet," Callie said dryly.

216

Jamie chuckled at the two of them. "If I know Percy, he's probably planning to spend more time with the lassies than with Dee," he said as Percy walked into the room. "Is that it, Percy? Are you planning to court some red-haired Scottish girls?"

Percy reddened. "Who told you about Alyssa?" he demanded. "I just met her at the Pump Room the other day. I thought I was being discreet." He looked around in surprise as they all laughed, then he cleared his throat. "James, I need to speak to you privately."

"Say whatever you want in front of Callie and Dee. They're family."

Percy glanced around, then loosened his cravat with his finger. "I don't want to be the bearer of bad news, James, but I saw Miss Bramley out walking with Captain Sinclair. I just thought you should know." He finished all in a rush. "I'm sorry."

Jamie laughed. "I'm delighted. I've already told Callie, but I'll share it with you two: I've been jilted. Miss Bramley has cried off and plans to marry Captain Sinclair."

Percy looked at Callie in confusion. "But I thought that Captain Sinclair and . . . and . . ."

"Callie?" Dee asked. "I thought that was a strange match when you told me about it. He just ain't for Callie."

"No, thank goodness," Callie said. "Now, we have news. You said Aunt Mary was in love—well, you were right. She's turned into a rank romantic." She and Dee proceeded to tell them about Aunt Mary and Lord Easton. "Isn't that a romantic ending?" she asked as she finished.

"Talk about a rank romantic," Jamie teased, "I don't know who's worse: you or Aunt Mary." He paused a moment. "Not to change the subject, but are we planning on going to the Rooms tonight?"

Percy reddened. "I told Alyssa I'd be there," he muttered. "I need to get ready. Are we all going?"

All agreeing, they drifted from the library, with Jamie saying he had to attend to one or two other things before the afternoon was over. As he left, Callie went up to her room behind Dee. She caught herself singing as she skipped up the stairs.

Chapter Fourteen

Jamie hadn't returned by the time the rest of the family was ready to go to the ball. Lord Easton, though still coughing, declared himself well enough to escort both Aunt Mary and Callie, with Dee and Percy tagging along. As soon as they arrived at the ball, Lord Easton and Aunt Mary found chairs along the side, while Percy went in search of the red-haired Alyssa. Dee wandered off on his own, leaving Callie standing close to a palm along the wall. She stood back against the wall, taking refuge behind the palm fronds. She wished Jamie had come back in time to be here. She had taken particular pains with her dress, adding some lace and ribbon trim she had bought in Milsom Street and had been saving for a special occasion. Even Brewster had been satisfied with her appearance.

Venetia came in through the door, wearing a cream dress trimmed with coquelicot ribbons. She was glowing and looked beautiful. Andrew Sinclair walked a step behind her, right beside her father, who, Callie thought, looked as hale and florid as ever. Callie moved farther back into the palm fronds, but Venetia had already spotted her. "Callie, my love," Venetia said, rushing down upon her, "it's so good to see you. How can I ever thank you?" She embraced Callie, then turned to Andrew. "Look, Andrew, it's Callie." Callie had the distinct impression that everyone in the ballroom was looking right at her.

Andrew bent low over her hand. "Thank you so much, Miss Stone. I'll be forever in your debt."

"Wonderful," stammered Callie, "that is, I'm glad to have been of any assistance."

"Callie, you can't believe how happy I am," Venetia said, patting Andrew's arm possessively. "I knew you would make things all right."

"And she certainly did, didn't she?"

Callie turned to see Jamie looking at her through the fronds. He was standing on the other side of the potted palm. She caught her breath. He was in evening dress and looked positively splendid. Andrew looked a pale stick figure in comparison. Jamie walked around the palm and stood beside her. "I'm delighted that everything worked out to satisfaction," Jamie said with a chuckle. "Now, if you will excuse us, I've a promise to keep." With that, he took Callie's hand and led her toward the door.

"Where are we going?"

"It's a surprise," he said with a smile at her. "Don't make me divulge anything too soon."

She paused at the door and looked around. "Do you want to leave the ball? I'll have to tell Aunt Mary so she'll know I've left with you. I don't want her to worry."

He gave her arm a tug. "She won't — I've already

told her you were going with me. I never leave my surprises with dangling ends. Well, almost never. Come on." He placed her shawl around her shoulders and led her outside and down the street to where a rather large coach was waiting. "I apologize for the coach and this excuse for horseflesh," he said as he handed her up. "Aunt Cavendish borrowed my carriage, and the curricle just wasn't what I wanted."

"Wanted for what?" she asked as they went creaking off down the street. "And where did you find this?"

"To answer in order—I wanted it for my surprise, and second, it belongs to Aunt Cavendish, and I do believe she must have inherited it from her grandfather or some such. It's ancient, and so are these spavined horses." He turned and smiled at her, and her heart gave a lurch. "But then, it's the thought that counts. Remember that." He started singing a sentimental ballad. Callie thought his behavior strange, but if he wanted to sing, that was fine with her. She did note that his singing was rather off-key, but reminded herself that it was the thought that counted.

He drove right up to the side of Sydney Gardens and stopped the coach beside some shrubbery. With great ceremony, and now humming the song, he helped Callie down. The Gardens were beautiful in the moonlight, and Callie looked around, taking in the scene. This was one of her favorite places in the daytime, but at night it was almost enchanted. She took a deep breath, drinking in the scent of the Gardens, then smelled something burning.

"You could pay attention," Jamie said irritably. "I'm trying to do this right, but you could help me a little. Keep in mind that I'm rather new at this." Callie turned around to see him placing a candle on the top of the wheel and trying unsuccessfully to light it. He swore as it kept toppling over.

"Let me hold it," she said, catching the candle as it almost fell. "There." He struck the flint and the candle caught, but it blew out immediately. He tried again, and this time held his hand around it until the flame burned steadily. "This is more difficult than I thought it would be," he said with a grin.

"What is?" Callie really wasn't thinking too much about what he was saying. She was fascinated by the picture he made in the moonlight. She had never seen a man so handsome. "What is?" she asked again, realizing she had missed his answer. He was beginning to sing the ballad again.

"You said you wanted a romantic man. Well, I'm trying to be romantic," he said, "but I own you're making it damned difficult. I'm having the devil's own time with all this music and candles. I wanted to hire a violinist but couldn't find one on short notice, so I'm reduced to humming and trying to sing by myself." He gave her a rueful grin. "There's got to be a better way." He sheltered the candle as a soft breeze blew by. "What I really wanted to do was to find a nice, romantic setting and ask you to marry me, but I seem to be making a botch of it."

"You want *me* to marry you?" Happiness flooded over her. "Jamie, is that what you said?"

"Yes, I want you to marry me." He forgot the candle and reached out to take her hand. "I love you very much, Callie, even if I'm not the most romantic man in the world. I'll always love you and be the best husband I can be. If you'll have me, I'll spend my whole life trying to make you happy." He paused. "That's not very romantic, but it's how I feel."

"That's the most romantic thing I've ever heard," she said, coming close to him and putting her arms around his neck. "I love you too, Jamie, I really do. I've loved you forever, I think."

He held her and kissed her lightly, then looked up as they heard the sound of a carriage going by. "Let's combine romance and practicality," he said, blowing out the candle flame and pulling her into the shadows between the shrubbery and the coach.

Then he gave her a long, most satisfactory, romantic kiss. "Jamie," Callie said at last, catching her breath, "if this is practicality, it's just fine."

REGENCY ROMANCES
Lords and Ladies in Love

A TOUCH OF VENUS   (3153, $3.95)
by Patricia Laye

Raines Scott knew she had to hide her youth and beauty to get the job cataloguing rare coins. The handsome Lord Kemp doubted the intellectual skills of *any* woman, and had less than scholarly pursuits on his mind when he realized his new employee's charms.

REGENCY MORNING   (3152, $2.95)
by Elizabeth Law

When their father died, leaving them alone and penniless, the St. John girls were at the mercy of their aloof and handsome cousin Tarquin. Laurie had planned the future for all of them, including her sister's marriage to Tarquin. Plans rarely work out as imagined, however, as Laurie realized when she lost her heart to her arrogant cousin.

DELIGHTFUL DECEPTION   (3053, $2.95)
by Nancy Lawrence

Outspoken Charmain Crewes fled from home to avoid the arranged match with the rakish Earl of Wexford. When her coachman fell ill, she hired the handsome stranger who was watching her in the woods. The Earl of Wexford was in no hurry to tell her he was exactly the man from whom she had run away, until her charms captured his heart!

THE DUCHESS AND THE DEVIL   (3279, $2.95)
by Sydney Ann Clark

Byrony Balmaine had promised her wealthy uncle to marry the man of his choosing. She never imagined Uncle Charles would choose the rakehell Deveril St. John, known as the Devil Duke by those who knew of his libertine ways. She vowed to keep her promise to her uncle, but she made another promise to herself: the handsome duke may claim her in matrimony, but he would never claim her heart. If only he weren't so dangerously handsome and charming . . .